SOLOMON JOHN'S BOOK

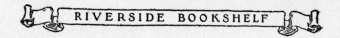

RIVERSIDE BOOKSHELF

THE PETERKIN PAPERS

BY

LUCRETIA P. HALE

WITH ILLUSTRATIONS IN COLOR

BY HAROLD BRETT

AND WITH CUTS IN THE TEXT

BOSTON AND NEW YORK
HOUGHTON MIFFLIN COMPANY
The Riverside Press Cambridge

The Riverside Press
CAMBRIDGE · MASSACHUSETTS
PRINTED IN THE U.S.A.

TO

MEGGIE

(THE DAUGHTER OF THE LADY FROM PHILADELPHIA)

TO WHOM THESE STORIES WERE FIRST TOLD

FOREWORD TO THE THIRD EDITION

PEOPLE who read this book will see that it is dedicated "to Meggie, — the daughter of the Lady from Philadelphia, — to whom these stories were first told."

Meggie remembers, as a very little girl, sitting up in bed in a clean little farmhouse room, with Aunt Lucretia, as she always called her, seated beside her and telling her the first story of them all. So that was the first time that any child ever heard about Mrs. Peterkin's troubles with her cup of coffee.

It seemed to Meggie, I know, the most natural thing in the world that Mrs. Lesley, the wise Lady from Philadelphia, should have brought these troubles to a fortunate end. For that was just what that dear mother of hers had always done, whenever she came across unlucky people, both in Philadelphia and out of it.

Later, Meggie's sister Mary listened to these stories, too, sitting on the steps of the farmhouse and looking off toward Mount Wachusett.

And I suppose their mother was there, and perhaps their father, Professor Peter Lesley, who was wise like his wife, and learned too. Very wise people usually feel more for foolish people, and understand them better, than people do who are only rather wise. This may be the reason why the Lesley family were the very earliest friends of the Peterkins.

ELLEN DAY HALE

PREFACE

THE first of these stories was accepted by Mr. Howard M. Ticknor for the "Young Folks" more than fifty years ago. They were afterwards continued in numbers of the "St. Nicholas."

The Peterkins originally hesitated about publishing their Family Papers, but were decided by referring the matter to the lady from Philadelphia. A little uncertain whether she might happen to be at Philadelphia, they determined to write and ask her.

Solomon John suggested a postal-card. Everybody reads a postal, and everybody would read it as it came along, and see its importance, and help it on. If the lady from Philadelphia were away, her family and all her servants would read it, and send it after her, for answer.

Elizabeth Eliza thought the postal a bright idea. It would not take so long to write as a letter, and would not be so expensive. But could they get the whole subject on a postal?

Mr. Peterkin believed there could be no difficulty, there was but one question: —

Shall the adventures of the Peterkin family be published?

This was decided upon, and there was room for each of the family to sign, the little boys contenting themselves with rough sketches of their india-rubber boots.

Mr. Peterkin, Agamemnon, and Solomon John took the postal-card to the post-office early one morning, and by the afternoon of that very day, and all the next day, and for many days, came streaming in answers on postals and in letters. Their card had been addressed to the lady from Philadelphia, with the number of her street. But it must have been read by their neighbors in their own town post-office before leaving; it must have been read along its way: for by each mail came piles of postals and letters from town after town, in answer to the question, and all in the same tone: "Yes, yes; publish the adventures of the Peterkin family."

"Publish them, of course."

And in time came the answer of the lady from Philadelphia: —

"Yes, of course; publish them."

This is why they were published.

CONTENTS.

———•———

CONTENTS.

ILLUSTRATIONS

Drawn by Harold Brett

THE PETERKIN PAPERS

THE LADY WHO PUT SALT IN HER COFFEE.

HIS was Mrs. Peterkin. It was a mistake. She had poured out a delicious cup of coffee, and, just as she was helping herself to cream, she found she had put in salt instead of sugar! It tasted bad. What should she do? Of course she couldn't drink the coffee; so she called in the family, for she was sitting at a late breakfast all alone. The family came in; they all tasted, and looked, and wondered what should be done, and all sat down to think.

At last Agamemnon, who had been to college, said, "Why don't we go over and ask the advice of the chemist?" (For the chemist lived over the way, and was a very wise man.)

Mrs. Peterkin said, "Yes," and Mr. Peterkin said, "Very well," and all the children said they would go too. So the little boys put on their india-rubber boots, and over they went.

Now the chemist was just trying to find out something which should turn everything it touched into gold; and he had a large glass bottle into which he put all kinds of gold and silver, and many other valuable things, and melted them all up over the fire, till he had almost found what he wanted. He could turn things into almost gold. But just now he had used up all the gold that he had round the house, and gold was high. He had used up his

wife's gold thimble and his great-grandfather's gold-bowed spectacles; and he had melted up the gold head of his great-great-grandfather's cane; and, just as the Peterkin family came in, he was down on his knees before his wife, asking her to let him have her wedding-ring to melt up with all the rest, because this time he knew he should succeed, and should be able to turn everything into gold; and then she could have a new wedding-ring of diamonds. all set in emeralds and rubies and topazes.

and all the furniture could be turned into the finest of gold.

Now his wife was just consenting when the Peterkin family burst in. You can imagine how mad the chemist was! He came near throwing his crucible — that was the name of his melting-pot — at their heads. But he didn't. He listened as calmly as he could to the story of how Mrs. Peterkin had put salt in her coffee.

At first he said he couldn't do anything about it; but when Agamemnon said they would pay in gold if he would only go, he packed up his bottles in a leather case, and went back with them all.

First he looked at the coffee, and then stirred it. Then he put in a little chlorate of potassium, and the family tried it all round; but it tasted no better. Then he stirred in a little bichlorate of magnesia. But Mrs. Peterkin didn't like that. Then he added some tartaric acid and some hypersulphate of lime. But no; it was no better. "I have it!" exclaimed the chemist, — "a little ammonia is just the thing!" No, it wasn't the thing at all.

Then he tried, each in turn, some oxalic, cyanic, acetic, phosphoric, chloric, hyperchloric, sulphuric, boracic, silicic, nitric, formic, nitrous nitric, and carbonic acids. Mrs. Peterkin tasted each, and said the flavor was pleasant, but not precisely that of coffee. So then he tried a little calcium, aluminum, barium, and strontium, a little clear bitumen, and a half of a third of a sixteenth of a grain of arsenic. This gave rather a pretty color; but still Mrs. Peterkin ungratefully said it tasted of anything but coffee. The chemist was not discouraged. He put in a little belladonna and atropine, some granulated hydrogen, some potash, and a very little antimony, finishing off with a little pure carbon. But still Mrs. Peterkin was not satisfied.

The chemist said that all he had done ought to have taken out the salt. The theory remained the same, although the experiment had failed. Perhaps a little starch would have some effect. If not, that was all the time he could give. He should like to be paid, and go. They were all much obliged to him, and willing to give him $1.37½ in gold. Gold was now 2.69¾, so Mr. Peterkin found in the newspaper. This gave Agamemnon a pretty little sum. He sat himself down to do it. But there was the coffee! All sat and thought awhile, till Elizabeth Eliza said, "Why don't we go to the herb-woman?" Elizabeth Eliza was the only daughter. She was named after her two aunts, — Elizabeth, from the sister of her father; Eliza, from her mother's sister. Now, the herb-woman was an old woman who came round to sell herbs, and knew a great deal. They all shouted with joy at the idea of asking her, and Solomon John and the younger children agreed to go and find her too. The herb-woman lived down at the very end of the street; so tne boys put on their india-rubber boots again, and they set off. It was a long walk through the village, but they came at last to the herb-woman's house, at the foot of a high hill. They went through her little garden. Here she had marigolds and holly-hocks, and old maids and tall sunflowers, and all kinds of sweet-smelling herbs, so that the air was full of tansy-tea and elder-blow.

Over the porch grew a hop-vine, and a brandy-cherry tree shaded the door, and a luxuriant cranberry-vine flung its delicious fruit across the window. They went into a small parlor, which smelt very spicy. All around hung little bags full of catnip, and peppermint, and all kinds of herbs; and dried stalks hung from the ceiling; and on the shelves were jars of rhubarb, senna, manna, and the like.

But there was no little old woman. She had gone up into the woods to get some more wild herbs, so they all thought they would follow her, — Elizabeth Eliza,

Solomon John, and the little boys. They had to climb up over high rocks, and in among huckleberry-bushes and black-berry-vines. But the little boys had their india-rubber boots. At last they discovered the little old woman. They knew her by her hat. It was steeple-crowned, without any vane. They saw her digging with her trowel round a sassafras bush. They told her their story, — how their mother had put salt in her coffee, and how the chemist had made it worse instead of better, and how their mother couldn't drink it, and wouldn't she come and see what she could do? And she said she would, and took up her little old apron, with pockets all round, all filled with everlasting and pennyroyal, and went back to her house.

There she stopped, and stuffed her huge pockets with some of all the kinds of herbs. She took some tansy and peppermint, and caraway-seed and dill, spearmint and cloves, pennyroyal and sweet marjoram, basil and rosemary, wild thyme and some of the other time, — such as you have in clocks, — sappermint and oppermint, catnip, valerian, and hop; indeed, there isn't a kind of herb you can think of that the little old woman didn't have done up in her little paper bags, that had all been dried in her little

Dutch-oven. She packed these all up, and then went back with the children, taking her stick.

Meanwhile Mrs. Peterkin was getting quite impatient for her coffee.

As soon as the little old woman came she had it set over the fire, and began to stir in the different herbs. First she put in a little hop for the bitter. Mrs. Peterkin said it tasted like hop-tea, and not at all like coffee. Then she tried a little flagroot and snakeroot, then some spruce gum, and some caraway and some dill, some rue and rosemary, some sweet marjoram and sour, some oppermint and sappermint, a little spearmint and peppermint, some wild thyme, and some of the other tame time, some tansy and basil, and catnip and valerian, and sassafras, ginger, and pennyroyal. The children tasted after each mixture, but made up dreadful faces. Mrs. Peterkin tasted, and did the same. The more the old woman stirred, and the more she put in, the worse it all seemed to taste.

So the old woman shook her head, and muttered a few words, and said she must go. She believed the coffee was bewitched. She bundled up her packets of herbs, and took  her trowel, and her basket, and her stick, and went back to her root of sassafras, that she had left half in the air and half out. And all she would take for pay was five cents in currency.

Then the family were in despair, and all sat and

thought a great while. It was growing late in the day,
and Mrs. Peterkin hadn t had her cup of coffee. At last
Elizabeth Eliza said, "They say that the lady from
Philadelphia, who is staying in town, is very wise. Suppose I go and ask her what is best to be done." To
this they all agreed, it was a great thought, and off
Elizabeth Eliza went.

She told the lady from Philadelphia the whole
story, — how her mother had put salt in the coffee; how
the chemist had been called in; how he tried everything
but could make it no better; and how they went for
the little old herb-woman, and how she had tried in
vain, for her mother couldn't drink the coffee. The
lady from Philadelphia listened very attentively, and
then said, "Why doesn't your mother make a fresh cup

of coffee?" Elizabeth Eliza
started with surprise. Solomon John shouted with
joy; so did Agamemnon,
who had just finished his
sum; so did the little boys,
who had followed on. "Why
didn't we think of that?"
said Elizabeth Eliza; and they all went back to their
mother, and she had her cup of coffee.

ABOUT ELIZABETH ELIZA'S PIANO.

LIZABETH ELIZA had a present of a piano, and she was to take lessons of the postmaster's daughter.

They decided to have the piano set across the window in the parlor, and the carters brought it in, and went away.

After they had gone the family all came in to look at the piano; but they found the carters had placed it with its back turned towards the middle of the room, standing close against the window.

How could Elizabeth Eliza open it? How could she reach the keys to play upon it?

Solomon J o h n proposed that they should open the window, which Agamemnon could do with his long arms. Then Elizabeth Eliza should go round upon the piazza, and open the piano. Then she could have

her music-stool on the piazza, and play upon the piano there.

So they tried this; and they all thought it was a very pretty sight to see Elizabeth Eliza playing on the piano, while she sat on the piazza, with the honeysuckle vines behind her.

It was very pleasant, too, moonlight evenings. Mr. Peterkin liked to take a doze on his sofa in the room; but the rest of the family liked to sit on the piazza. So did Elizabeth Eliza, only she had to have her back to the moon.

All this did very well through the summer; but, when the fall came, Mr. Peterkin thought the air was too cold from the open window, and the family did not want to sit out on the piazza.

Elizabeth Eliza practised in the mornings with her

cloak on; but she was obliged to give up her music in the evenings the family shivered so.

One day, when she was talking with the lady from Philadelphia, she spoke of this trouble.

The lady from Philadelphia looked surprised, and then said, "But why don't you turn the piano round?"

One of the little boys pertly said, "It is a square piano."

But Elizabeth Eliza went home directly, and, with the

ELIZABETH ELIZA'S PIANO

help of Agamemnon and Solomon John, turned the piano round.

"Why did we not think of that before?" said Mrs. Peterkin. "What shall we do when the lady from Philadelphia goes home again?"

THE PETERKINS TRY TO BECOME WISE.

HEY were sitting round the break-fast-table, and wondering what they should do because the lady from Philadelphia had gone away. "If," said Mrs. Peterkin, "we could only be more wise as a family!" How could they manage it? Agamemnon had been to college, and the children all went to school; but still as a family they were not wise. "It comes from books," said one of the family. "People who have a great many books are very wise." Then they counted up that there were very few books in the house, — a few school-books and Mrs. Peterkin's cook-book were all.

"That's the thing!" said Agamemnon. "We want a library."

"We want a library!" said Solomon John. And all of them exclaimed, "We want a library!"

"Let us think how we shall

get one," said Mrs. Peterkin. "I have observed that other people think a great deal of thinking."

So they all sat and thought a great while.

Then said Agamemnon, "I will make a library. There are some boards in the wood-shed, and I have a hammer and some nails, and perhaps we can borrow some hinges, and there we have our library!"

They were all very much pleased at the idea.

"That's the bookcase part," said Elizabeth Eliza; "but where are the books?"

So they sat and thought a little while, when Solomon John exclaimed, "I will make a book!"

They all looked at him in wonder.

"Yes," said Solomon John, "books will make us wise; but first I must make a book."

So they went into the parlor, and sat down to make a book. But there was no ink. What should he do for ink? Elizabeth Eliza said she had heard that nutgalls and vinegar made very good ink. So they decided to make some. The little boys said they could find some nutgalls up in the woods. So they all agreed to set out and pick some. Mrs. Peterkin put on her cape-bonnet, and the little boys got into their india-rubber boots, and off they went.

The nutgalls were hard to find. There was almost everything else in the woods, — chestnuts and walnuts, and small hazel-nuts, and a great many squirrels; and they had to walk a great way before they found any nutgalls. At last they came home with a large basket and two nutgalls in it. Then came the question of the vinegar. Mrs. Peterkin had used her very last on some beets they had the day before. "Suppose we go and ask the minister's wife," said Elizabeth Eliza. So they all went to the minister's wife. She said if they wanted some good vinegar they had better set a barrel of cider down in the cellar, and in a year or two it would make very nice vinegar. But they said they wanted it that very afternoon. When the minister's wife heard this she said she should be very glad to let them have some vinegar, and gave them a cupful to carry home.

So they stirred in the nutgalls, and by the time evening came they had very good ink.

Then Solomon John wanted a pen. Agamemnon had a steel one, but Solomon John said, "Poets always used quills." Elizabeth Eliza suggested that they should go out to the poultry-yard and get a quill. But it was already dark. They had, however, two lanterns, and the little boys borrowed the neighbors'. They set out in procession for the poultry-yard. When they got there the fowls were all at roost, so they could look at them quietly. But there were no geese! There were Shanghais, and Cochin-Chinas, and Guinea hens, and Barbary hens, and speckled hens, and Poland roosters, and bantams, and ducks, and turkeys, but not one goose! "No geese but ourselves," said Mrs. Peterkin, wittily, as they returned to the house. The sight of this procession roused up the village. "A torch-light procession!" cried all the boys of the town; and they gathered round the house, shouting for the flag; and Mr. Peterkin had to invite them in, and give them cider and gingerbread, before he could explain to them that it was only his family visiting his hens.

After the crowd had dis-persed Solomon John sat down to think of his writing again. Agamemnon agreed to go over to the bookstore to get a quill. They all went over with him. The book-seller was just shutting up his shop. However, he agreed to go in and get a quill, which he did, and they hur-ried home.

So Solomon John sat down again, but there was no paper. And now the bookstore was shut up. Mr. Peterkin suggested that the mail was about in, and perhaps he should have a letter, and then they could use the envelope

to write upon. So they all went to the post-office, and
the little boys had their india-rubber boots on, and they
all shouted when they found Mr. Peterkin had a letter.
The postmaster inquired what they were shouting about;
and when they told him he said he would give Solomon
John a whole sheet of paper for his book. And they all
went back rejoicing.

So Solomon John sat
down, and the family all sat
round the table looking at
him. He had his pen, his ink,
and his paper. He dipped
his pen into the ink and held it over the paper,
and thought a minute, and then said, "But I haven't got
anything to say."

MRS. PETERKIN WISHES TO GO TO DRIVE.

 NE morning Mrs. Peterkin was feeling very tired, as she had been having a great many things to think of, and she said to Mr. Peterkin, "I believe I shall take a ride this morning!"

And the little boys cried out, "Oh, may we go too?"

Mrs. Peterkin said that Elizabeth Eliza and the little boys might go.

So Mr. Peterkin had the horse put into the carryall, and he and Agamemnon went off to their business, and Solomon John to school; and Mrs. Peterkin began to get ready for her ride.

She had some currants she wanted to carry to old Mrs. Twomly, and some gooseberries for somebody else, and Elizabeth Eliza wanted to pick some flowers to take to the minister's wife; so it took them a long time to prepare.

The little boys went out to pick the currants and the gooseberries, and Elizabeth Eliza went out for her flowers, and Mrs. Peterkin put on her cape-bonnet, and in time they were all ready. The little boys were in their india-rubber boots, and they got into the carriage.

Elizabeth Eliza was to drive; so she sat on the front seat, and took up the reins, and the horse started off merrily, and then suddenly stopped, and would not go any farther.

Elizabeth Eliza shook the reins, and pulled them, and then she clucked to the horse; and Mrs. Peterkin clucked; and the little boys whistled and shouted; but still the horse would not go.

"We shall have to whip him," said Elizabeth Eliza.

Now Mrs. Peterkin never liked to use the whip; but, as the horse would not go, she said she would get out and turn his head the other way, while Elizabeth Eliza whipped the horse, and when he began to go she would hurry and get in.

So they tried this, but the horse would not stir.

"Perhaps we have too heavy a load," said Mrs. Peterkin, as she got in.

So they took out the currants and the gooseberries and the flowers, but still the horse would not go.

One of the neighbors, from the opposite house, looking out just then, called out to them to try the whip. There was a high wind, and they could not hear exactly what she said.

"I have tried the whip," said Elizabeth Eliza.

"She says 'whips,' such as you eat," said one of the little boys.

"We might make those," said Mrs. Peterkin, thoughtfully.

"We have got plenty of cream," said Elizabeth Eliza.

"Yes, let us have some whips," cried the little boys, getting out.

And the opposite neighbor cried out something about whips; and the wind was very high.

So they went into the kitchen, and whipped up the cream, and made some very delicious whips; and the little boys tasted all round, and they all thought they were very nice.

They carried some out to the horse, who swallowed it down very quickly.

"That is just what he wanted," said Mrs. Peterkin; "now he will certainly go!"

So they all got into the carriage again, and put in the currants, and the gooseberries, and the flowers; and Elizabeth Eliza shook the reins, and they  all clucked; but still the horse would not go!

"We must either give up our ride," said Mrs.

Peterkin, mournfully, "or else send over to the lady from
Philadelphia, and see what she will say."

The little boys jumped out as quickly as they
could; they were eager to go and ask the lady from
Philadelphia. Elizabeth Eliza went with them, while her
mother took the reins.

They found that the lady from Philadelphia was very
ill that day, and was in her bed. But when she was
told what the trouble was she very kindly said they might

draw up the curtain from the
window at the foot of the
bed, and open the blinds,
and she would see. Then
she asked for her opera-
glass, and looked through
it, across the way, up the

street, to Mrs. Peterkin's door.

After she had looked through the glass she laid it
down, leaned her head back against the pillow, for she
was very tired, and then said, "Why don't you unchain
the horse from the horse-post?"

Elizabeth Eliza and the little boys looked at one
another, and then hurried back to the house and told
their mother. The horse was untied, and they all went
to ride.

THE PETERKINS AT HOME.

AT DINNER.

A NOTHER little incident occurred in the Peterkin family. This was at dinner-time.

They sat down to a dish of boiled ham. Now it was a peculiarity of the children of the family that half of them liked fat, and half liked lean. Mr. Peterkin sat down to cut the ham. But the ham turned out to be a very remarkable one. The fat and the lean came in separate slices,— first one of lean, then one of fat, then two slices of lean, and so on. Mr. Peterkin began as usual by helping the children first, according to their age. Now Agamemnon, who liked lean, got a fat slice; and Elizabeth Eliza, who preferred fat, had a lean slice. Solomon John, who could eat nothing but lean, was helped to fat, and so on. Nobody had what he could eat.

It was a rule of the Peterkin family that no one should eat any of the vegetables without some of the meat; so now, although the children saw upon their plates apple-sauce, and squash and tomato, and sweet potato and sour potato, not one of them could eat a mouthful, because not one was satisfied with the meat. Mr. and Mrs. Peterkin, however, liked both fat and lean, and were making a very good meal, when they looked up and saw the children all sitting eating nothing, and looking dissatisfied into their plates.

"What is the matter now?" said Mr. Peterkin.

But the children were taught not to speak at table. Agamemnon, however, made a sign of disgust at his fat, and Elizabeth Eliza at her lean, and so on; and they presently discovered what was the difficulty.

"What shall be done now?" said Mrs. Peterkin.

They all sat and thought for a little while.

At last said Mrs. Peterkin, rather uncertainly, "Suppose we ask the lady from Philadelphia what is best to be done."

But Mr. Peterkin said he didn't like to go to her for everything; let the children try and eat their dinner as it was.

And they all tried, but they couldn't. "Very well, then," said Mr. Peterkin, "let them go and ask the lady from Philadelphia."

"All of us?" cried one of the little boys, in the excitement of the moment.

"Yes," said Mrs. Peterkin, "only put on your india-rubber boots." And they hurried out of the house.

The lady from Philadelphia was just going in to her dinner; but she kindly stopped in the entry to hear what the trouble was. Agamemnon and Elizabeth Eliza told her all the difficulty, and the lady from Philadelphia said, "But why don't you give the slices of fat to those who like the fat, and the slices of lean to those who like the lean?"

They looked at one another. Agamemnon looked at Elizabeth Eliza, and Solomon John looked at the little boys. "Why didn't we think of that?" said they, and ran home to tell their mother.

WHY THE PETERKINS HAD A LATE DINNER

HE trouble was in the dumb-waiter. All had seated themselves at the dinner table, and Amanda had gone to take out the dinner she had sent up from the kitchen on the dumb-waiter. But something was the matter; she could not pull it up. There was the dinner, but she could not reach it. All the family, in turn, went and tried; all pulled together in vain; the dinner could not be stirred.

"No dinner!" exclaimed Agamemnon.

"I am quite hungry," said Solomon John.

At last Mr. Peterkin said, "I am not proud. I am willing to dine in the kitchen."

This room was below the dining-room. All consented to this. Each one went down, taking a napkin.

The cook laid the kitchen table, put on it her best table-cloth, and the family sat down. Amanda went to the dumb-waiter for the dinner, but she could not move it down.

The family were all in dismay. There was the dinner,

half-way between the kitchen and dining-room, and there
were they all hungry to eat it!

"What is there for
dinner?" asked Mr. Peter-
kin.

"Roast turkey," said
Mrs. Peterkin.

Mr. Peterkin lifted his
eyes to the ceiling.

"Squash, tomato, potato, and sweet potato," Mrs.
Peterkin continued.

"Sweet potato!" exclaimed both the little boys.

"I am very glad now that I did not have cranberry,"
said Mrs. Peterkin, anxious to find a bright point.

"Let us sit down and think about it," said Mr. Peterkin.

"I have an idea," said Agamemnon, after a while.

"Let us hear it," said Mr. Peterkin. "Let each one
speak his mind."

"The turkey," said Agamemnon, "must be just above
the kitchen door. If I had a ladder and an axe, I could
cut away the plastering and reach it."

"That is a great idea," said Mrs. Peterkin.

"If you think you could do it," said Mr. Peterkin.

"Would it not be better to have a carpenter?" asked
Elizabeth Eliza.

"A carpenter might have a ladder and an axe, and
I think we have neither," said Mrs. Peterkin.

"A carpenter! A carpenter!" exclaimed the rest.

It was decided that Mr. Peterkin, Solomon John, and the little boys should go in search of a carpenter.

Agamemnon proposed that, meanwhile, he should go and borrow a book, for he had another idea.

"This affair of the turkey," he said, "reminds me of those buried cities that have been dug out, — Herculaneum for instance."

"Oh, yes," interrupted Elizabeth Eliza, "and Pompeii."

"Yes," said Agamemnon. "They found there pots

and kettles. Now, I should like to know how they did it; and I mean to borrow a book and read. I think it was done with a pickaxe."

So the party set out. But when Mr. Peterkin reached the carpenter's shop there was no carpenter to be found there.

"He must be at his house, eating his dinner," suggested Solomon John.

"Happy man," exclaimed Mr. Peterkin, "he has a dinner to eat!"

They went to the carpenter's house, but found he had gone out of town for a day's job. But his wife told them that he always came back at night to ring the nine-o'clock bell.

"We must wait till then," said Mr. Peterkin, with an effort at cheerfulness.

At home he found Agamemnon reading his book, and all sat down to hear of Herculaneum and Pompeii.

Time passed on, and the question arose about tea. Would it do to have tea when they had had no dinner? A part of the family thought it would not do; the rest wanted tea.

"I suppose you remember the wise lady of Philadelphia, who was here not long ago?" said Mr. Peterkin.

"Oh, yes," said Mrs. Peterkin.

"Let us try to think what she would advise us," said Mr. Peterkin.

"I wish she were here," said Elizabeth Eliza.

"I think," said Mr. Peterkin, "she would say, let them that want tea have it; the rest can go without."

So they had tea, and, as it proved, all sat down to it. But not much was eaten, as there had been no dinner.

When the nine-o'clock bell was heard, Agamemnon, Solomon John, and the little boys rushed to the church and found the carpenter.

They asked him to bring a ladder, axe, and pickaxe. As he felt it might be a case of fire he brought also his fire-buckets.

When the matter was explained to him he went into the dining-room, looked into the dumb-waiter, untwisted a cord, and arranged the weight, and pulled up the dinner.

There was a family shout.

"The trouble was in the weight," said the carpenter.

"That is why it is called a dumb-waiter," Solomon John explained to the little boys.

The dinner was put upon the table.

Mrs. Peterkin frugally suggested that they might now keep it for next day, as to-day was almost gone, and they had had tea.

But nobody listened. All sat down to the roast turkey, and Amanda warmed over the vegetables.

"Patient waiters are no losers," said Agamemnon.

THE PETERKINS' SUMMER JOURNEY.

 FACT, it was their last summer's journey, — for it had been planned then; but there had been so many difficulties it had been delayed.

The first trouble had been about trunks. The family did not own a trunk suitable for travelling. Agamemnon had his valise, that he had used when he stayed a week at a time at the academy; and a trunk had been bought for Elizabeth Eliza when she went to the seminary. Solomon John and Mr. Peterkin, each had his patent-leather hand-bag. But all these were too small for the family. And the little boys wanted to carry their kite.

Mrs. Peterkin suggested her grandmother's trunk. This was a hair-trunk, very large and capacious. It would hold everything they would want to carry except what would go in Elizabeth Eliza's trunk, or the valise and bags.

Everybody was delighted at this idea. It was agreed that the next day the things should be brought into Mrs. Peterkin's room for her to see if they could all be packed.

"If we can get along," said Elizabeth Eliza, "without having to ask advice I shall be glad!"

"Yes," said Mr. Peterkin, "it is time now for people to be coming to ask advice of us."

The next morning Mrs. Peterkin began by taking out

the things that were already in the trunk. Here were last year's winter things, and not only these, but old clothes that had been put away,— Mrs. Peterkin's wedding-dress; the skirts the little boys used to wear before they put on jackets and trousers.

All day Mrs. Peterkin worked over the trunk, putting away the old things, putting in the new. She packed up all the clothes she could think of, both summer and winter ones, because you never can tell what sort of weather you will have.

Agamemnon fetched his books, and Solomon John his spy-glass. There were her own and Elizabeth Eliza's best bonnets in a bandbox; also Solomon John's hats, for he had an old one and a new one. He bought a new hat for fishing, with a very wide brim and deep crown; all of heavy straw.

Agamemnon brought down a large heavy dictionary, and an atlas still larger. This contained maps of all the countries in the world.

"I have never had a chance to look at them," he said; "but when one travels, then is the time to study geography."

Mr. Peterkin wanted to take his turning-lathe. So Mrs. Peterkin packed his tool-chest. It gave her some trouble, for it came to her just as she had packed her summer dresses. At first she thought it would help to smooth the dresses, and placed it on top; but she was forced to take all out, and set it at the bottom. This was not so much matter, as she had not yet the right dresses to put in. Both Mrs. Peterkin and

Elizabeth Eliza would need new dresses for this occasion. The little boys' hoops went in; so did their india-rubber boots, in case it should not rain when they started. They each had a hoe and shovel, and some baskets, that were packed.

Mrs. Peterkin called in all the family on the evening of the second day to see how she had succeeded. Everything was packed, even the little boys' kite lay smoothly on the top.

"I like to see a thing so nicely done," said Mr. Peterkin.

The next thing was to cord up the trunk, and Mr. Peterkin tried to move it. But neither he, nor Ags

memnon, nor Solomon John could lift it alone, or all
together.

Here was a serious difficulty. Solomon John tried to
make light of it.

"Expressmen could lift it. Expressmen were used to
such things."

"But we did not plan expressing it," said Mrs.
Peterkin, in a discouraged tone.

"We can take a carriage," said Solomon John.

"I am afraid the trunk would not go on the back
of a car-
riage,"
said Mrs.
Peterkin.
"The
hackman

could not lift it, either," said Mr. Peterkin.

"People do travel with a great deal of baggage,"
said Elizabeth Eliza.

"And with very large trunks," said Agamemnon.

"Still they are trunks that can be moved," said Mr.
Peterkin, giving another try at the trunk in vain. "I
am afraid we must give it up," he said; "it would be
such a trouble in going from place to place."

"We would not mind if we got it to the place,"
said Elizabeth Eliza.

"But how to get it there?" Mr. Peterkin asked,
with a sigh.

"This is our first obstacle," said Agamemnon; "we must do our best to conquer it."

"What is an obstacle?" asked the little boys.

"It is the trunk," said Solomon John.

"Suppose we look out the word in the dictionary," said Agamemnon, taking the large volume from the trunk. "Ah, here it is" — And he read: —

"OBSTACLE, *an impediment.*"

"That is a worse word than the other," said one of the little boys.

"But listen to this," and Agamemnon continued: "*Impediment* is something that entangles the feet; *obstacle* something that stands in the way; *obstruction*, something that blocks up the passage; *hinderance*, something that holds back."

"The trunk is all these," said Mr. Peterkin, gloomily.

"It does not entangle the feet," said Solomon John, "for it can't move."

"I wish it could," said the little boys together.

Mrs. Peterkin spent a day or two in taking the things out of the trunk and putting them away.

"At least," she said, "this has given me some experience in packing."

And the little boys felt as if they had quite been a journey.

But the family did not like to give up their plan. It was suggested that they might take the things out of the trunk, and pack it at the station; the little boys could go and come with the things. But Elizabeth Eliza thought the place too public.

Gradually the old contents of the great trunk went back again to it.

At length a friend unexpectedly offered to lend Mr. Peterkin a good-sized family trunk. But it was late in the season, and so the journey was put off from that summer.

But now the trunk was sent round to the house, and a family consultation was held about packing it. Many things would have to be left at home, it was so much smaller than the grandmother's hair-trunk. But Agamemnon had been studying the atlas through the winter, and felt familiar with the more important places, so it would not be necessary to take it. And Mr. Peterkin decided to leave his turning-lathe at home, and his tool-chest.

Again Mrs. Peterkin spent two days in accommodating the things. With great care and discretion, and by borrowing two more leather bags, it could be accomplished. Everything of importance could be packed except the little boys' kite. What should they do about that?

The little boys proposed carrying it in their hands; but Solomon John and Elizabeth Eliza would not consent to this.

"I do think it is one of the cases where we might ask the advice of the lady from Philadelphia," said Mrs. Peterkin, at last.

"She has come on here," said Agamemnon, "and we have not been to see her this summer."

"She may think we have been neglecting her," suggested Mr. Peterkin.

The little boys begged to be allowed to go and ask her opinion about the kite. They came back in high spirits.

"She says we might leave this one at home, and make a new kite when we get there," they cried.

"What a sensible idea!" exclaimed Mr. Peterkin; "and I may have leisure to help you."

"We'll take plenty of newspapers," said Solomon John.

"And twine," said the little boys. And this matter was settled.

The question then was, "When should they go?"

THE PETERKINS SNOWED-UP.

MRS. PETERKIN awoke one morning to find a heavy snow-storm raging. The wind had flung the snow against the windows, had heaped it up around the house, and thrown it into huge white drifts over the fields, covering hedges and fences.

Mrs. Peterkin went from one window to the other to look out; but nothing could be seen but the driving storm and the deep white snow. Even Mr. Bromwick's house, on the opposite side of the street, was hidden by the swift-falling flakes.

"What shall I do about it?" thought Mrs. Peterkin. "No roads cleared out! Of course there'll be no butcher and no milkman!"

The first thing to be done was to wake up all the family early; for there was enough in the house for breakfast, and there was no knowing when they would have anything more to eat.

It was best to secure the breakfast first.

So she went from one room to the other, as soon as it was light, waking the family, and before long all were dressed and downstairs.

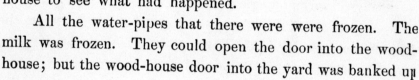

And then all went round the house to see what had happened.

All the water-pipes that there were were frozen. The milk was frozen. They could open the door into the wood-house; but the wood-house door into the yard was banked up

with snow; and the front door, and the piazza door, and the side door stuck. Nobody could get in or out!

Meanwhile, Amanda, the cook, had succeeded in making the kitchen fire, but had discovered there was no furnace coal.

"The furnace coal was to have come to-day," said Mrs. Peterkin, apologetically.

"Nothing will come to-day," said Mr. Peterkin, shivering.

But a fire could be made in a stove in the dining-room.

All were glad to sit down to breakfast and hot
coffee. The little boys were much pleased to have "ice-
cream" for breakfast.

"When we get a little warm," said Mr.
Peterkin, "we will consider what is to be
done."

"I am thankful I ordered the sausages
yesterday," said Mrs. Peterkin. "I was to
have had a leg of mutton to-day."

"Nothing will come to-day," said Agamemnon, gloomily.

"Are these sausages the last meat in the
house?" asked Mr. Peterkin.

"Yes," said Mrs. Peterkin.

The potatoes also were gone, the barrel of apples
empty, and she had meant to order more flour that very
day.

"Then we are eating our last provisions," said Solomon John, helping himself to another sausage.

"I almost wish we had stayed in bed," said Agamemnon.

"I thought it best to make sure of our breakfast first,"
repeated Mrs. Peterkin.

"Shall we literally have nothing left to eat?" asked Mr
Peterkin.

"There's the pig!" suggested Solomon John.

Yes, happily, the pigsty was at the end of the wood-
house, and could be reached under cover.

But some of the family could not eat fresh pork.

"We should have to 'corn' part of him," said Agamemnon.

"My butcher has always told me," said Mrs. Peterkin, "that if I wanted a ham I must keep a pig. Now we have the pig, but have not the ham!"

"Perhaps we could 'corn' one or two of his legs," suggested one of the little boys.

"We need not settle that now," said Mr. Peterkin. "At least the pig will keep us from starving."

The little boys looked serious; they were fond of their pig.

"If we had only decided to keep a cow," said Mrs. Peterkin.

"Alas! yes," said Mr. Peterkin, "one learns a great many things too late!"

"Then we might have had ice-cream all the time!" exclaimed the little boys.

Indeed, the little boys, in spite of the prospect of starving, were quite pleasantly excited at the idea of being snowed-up, and hurried through their breakfasts that they might go and try to shovel out a path from one of the doors.

"I ought to know more about the water-pipes," said Mr. Peterkin. "Now, I shut off the water last night in the bath-room, or else I forgot to; and I ought to have shut it off in the cellar."

The little boys came back. Such a wind at the front door, they were going to try the side door.

"Another thing I have learned to-day," said Mr. Peterkin, "is not to have all the doors on one side of the house, because the storm blows the snow against *all* the doors."

Solomon John started up.

"Let us see if we are blocked up on the east side of the house!" he exclaimed.

"Of what use," asked Mr. Peterkin, "since we have no door on the east side?"

"We could cut one," said Solomon John.

"Yes, we could cut a door," exclaimed Agamemnon.

"But how can we tell whether there is any snow there?" asked Elizabeth Eliza, — "for there is no window."

In fact, the east side of the Peterkins' house formed a blank wall. The owner had originally planned a little block of semi-detached houses. He had completed only one, very semi and very detached.

"It is not necessary to see," said Agamemnon, profoundly; "of course, if the storm blows against this side of the house, the house itself must keep the snow from the other side."

"Yes," said Solomon John, "there must be a space clear of snow on the east side of the house, and if we could open a way to that" —

"We could open a way to the butcher," said Mr. Peterkin, promptly.

Agamemnon went for his pickaxe. He had kept one in the house ever since the adventure of the dumb-waiter.

"What part of the wall had we better attack?" asked Mr. Peterkin.

Mrs. Peterkin was alarmed.

"What will Mr. Mudge, the owner of the house, think of it?" she exclaimed. "Have we a right to injure the wall of the house?"

"It is right to preserve ourselves from starving," said Mr. Peterkin. "The drowning man must snatch at a straw!"

"It is better that he should find his house chopped a little when the thaw comes," said Elizabeth Eliza, "than that he should find us lying about the house, dead of hunger, upon the floor."

Mrs. Peterkin was partially convinced.

The little boys came in to warm their hands. They had not succeeded in opening the side door, and were planning trying to open the door from the wood-house to the garden.

"That would be of no use," said Mrs. Peterkin, "the butcher cannot get into the garden."

"But we might shovel off the snow," suggested one of the little boys, "and dig down to some of last year's onions."

Meanwhile, Mr. Peterkin, Agamemnon, and Solomon

John had been bringing together their carpenter's tools, and Elizabeth Eliza proposed using a gouge, if they would choose the right spot to begin.

The little boys were delighted with the plan, and hastened to find, — one, a little hatchet, and the other a gimlet. Even Amanda armed herself with a poker.

"It would be better to begin on the ground floor," said Mr. Peterkin.

"Except that we may meet with a stone foundation," said Solomon John.

"If the wall is thinner upstairs," said Agamemnon, "it will do as well to cut a window as a door, and haul up anything the butcher may bring below in his cart."

Everybody began to pound a little on the wall to find a favorable place, and there was a great deal of noise. The little boys actually cut a bit out of the plastering with their hatchet and gimlet. Solomon John confided to Elizabeth Eliza that it reminded him of stories of prisoners  who cut themselves free, through stone walls, after days and days of secret labor.

Mrs. Peterkin, even, had come with a pair of tongs in her hand. She was interrupted by a voice behind her.

"Here's your leg of mutton, marm!"

It was the butcher. How had he got in?

"Excuse me, marm, for coming in at the side door, but the back gate is kinder blocked up. You were making such a pounding I could not make anybody hear me knock at the side door."

"But how did you make a path to the door?" asked Mr. Peterkin. "You must have been working at it a long time. It must be near noon now."

"I'm about on regular time," answered the butcher. "The town team has  cleared out the high road, and the wind has been down the last half-hour. The storm is over."

True enough! The Peterkins had been so busy inside the house they had not noticed the ceasing of the storm outside.

"And we were all up an hour earlier than usual," said Mr. Peterkin, when the butcher left. He had not explained to the butcher why he had a pickaxe in his hand.

"If we had lain abed till the usual time," said Solomon John, "we should have been all right."

"For here is the milkman!" said Elizabeth Eliza, as a knock was now heard at the side door.

"It is a good thing to learn," said Mr. Peterkin, "not to get up any earlier than is necessary."

THE PETERKINS DECIDE TO KEEP A COW.

OT that they were fond of drinking milk, nor that they drank very much. But for that reason Mr. Peterkin thought it would be well to have a cow, to encourage the family to drink more, as he felt it would be so healthy.

Mrs. Peterkin recalled the troubles of the last cold winter, and how near they came to starving, when they were shut up in a severe snowstorm, and the water-pipes burst, and the milk was frozen. If the cow-shed could open out of the wood-shed such trouble might be prevented.

Tony Larkin was to come over and milk the cow every morning, and Agamemnon and Solomon John agreed to learn how to milk, in case Tony should be "snowed up," or have the whooping-cough in the course of the winter. The little boys thought they knew how already.

But if they were to have three or four pailfuls of milk every day it was important to know where to keep it.

"One way will be," said Mrs. Peterkin, "to use a great deal every day. We will make butter."

"That will be admirable," thought Mr. Peterkin.

"And custards," suggested Solomon John.

"And syllabub," said Elizabeth Eliza.

"And cocoa-nut cakes," exclaimed the little boys.

"We don't need the milk for cocoa-nut cakes," said Mrs. Peterkin.

The little boys thought they might have a cocoa-nut tree instead of a cow. You could have the milk from the cocoanuts, and it would be pleasant climbing the tree, and you would not have to feed it.

"Yes," said Mr. Peterkin, "we shall have to feed the cow."

"Where shall we pasture her?" asked Agamemnon.

"Up on the hills, up on the hills," exclaimed the little boys, "where there are a great many bars to take down, and huckleberry-bushes!"

Mr. Peterkin had been thinking of their own little lot behind the house.

"But I don't know," he said, "but the cow might eat off all the grass in one day, and there would not be any left for to-morrow, unless the grass grew fast enough every night."

Agamemnon said it would depend upon the season. In a rainy season the grass would come up very fast, in a drought it might not grow at all.

"I suppose," said Mrs. Peterkin, "that is the worst of having a cow, — there might be a drought."

Mr. Peterkin thought they might make some calculation from the quantity of grass in the lot.

Solomon John suggested that measurements might be made by seeing how much grass the Bromwicks' cow, opposite them, eat up in a day.

The little boys agreed to go over and spend the day on the Bromwicks' fence, and take an observation.

"The trouble would be," said Elizabeth Eliza, "that cows walk about so, and the Bromwicks' yard is very large. Now she would be eating in one place, and then she would walk to another. She would not be eating all the time; a part of the time she would be chewing."

The little boys thought they should like nothing better than to have some sticks, and keep the cow in one corner of the yard till the calculations were made.

But Elizabeth Eliza was afraid the Bromwicks would not like it.

"Of course, it would bring all the boys in the school about the place, and very likely they would make the cow angry."

Agamemnon recalled that Mr. Bromwick once wanted to hire Mr. Peterkin's lot for his cow.

Mr. Peterkin started up.

THE LITTLE BOYS AGREED TO GO OVER AND SPEND THE DAY ON THE
BROMWICKS' FENCE, AND TAKE AN OBSERVATION

"That is true; and of course Mr. Bromwick must have known there was feed enough for one cow."

"And the reason you didn't let him have it," said Solomon John, "was that Elizabeth Eliza was afraid of cows."

"I did not like the idea," said Elizabeth Eliza, "of their cow's looking at me over the top of the fence, perhaps, when I should be planting the sweet peas in the garden. I hope our cow would be a quiet one. I should not like her jumping over the fence into the flower-beds."

Mr. Peterkin declared that he should buy a cow of the quietest kind.

"I should think something might be done about covering her horns," said Mrs. Peterkin; "that seems the most dangerous part. Perhaps they might be padded with cotton."

Elizabeth Eliza said cows were built so large and clumsy that if they came at you they could not help knocking you over.

The little boys would prefer having the pasture a great way off. Half the fun of having a cow would be going up on the hills after her.

Agamemnon thought the feed was not so good on the hills.

" The cow would like it ever so much better," the little boys declared, " on account of the variety. If she did not

like the rocks and the bushes she could walk round and find the grassy places."

" I am not sure," said Elizabeth Eliza, " but it would be less dan· gerous to keep the cow in the lot behind the house, because she would not be coming and going, morning and night, in that jerky way the Larkins' cows come home. They don't mind which gate they rush in at. I should hate to have our cow dash into our front yard just as I was coming home of an afternoon."

" That is true," said Mr. Peterkin; " we can have the door of the cow-house open directly into the pasture, and save the coming and going."

The little boys were quite disappointed. The cow would miss the exercise, and they would lose a great pleasure.

Solomon John suggested that they might sit on the fence and watch the cow.

It was decided to keep the cow in their own pasture; and, as they were to put on an end kitchen, it would be perfectly easy to build a dairy.

The cow proved a quiet one. She was a little excited when all the family stood round at the first milking, and watched her slowly walking into the shed.

Elizabeth Eliza had her scarlet sack dyed brown a fortnight before. It was the one she did her gardening in, and it might have infuriated the cow. And she kept out of the garden the first day or two.

Mrs. Peterkin and Elizabeth Eliza bought the best kind of milk-pans, of every size.

But there was a little disappointment about the taste of the milk.

The little boys liked it, and drank large mugs of it. Elizabeth Eliza said she could never learn to love milk warm from the cow, though she would like to do her best to patronize the cow.

Mrs. Peterkin was afraid Amanda did not understand about taking care of the milk; yet she had been down to overlook her, and she was sure the pans and the closet were all clean.

"Suppose we send a pitcher of cream over to the lady from Philadelphia to try," said Elizabeth Eliza; "it will be a pretty attention before she goes."

"It might be awkward if she didn't like it," said Solomon John. "Perhaps something is the matter with the grass."

"I gave the cow an apple to eat yesterday," said one of the little boys, remorsefully.

Elizabeth Eliza went over. and Mrs. Peterkin, too, and

explained all to the lady from Philadelphia, asking her to taste the milk.

The lady from Philadelphia tasted, and said the truth was that the milk was sour.

"I was afraid it was so," said Mrs. Peterkin; "but I didn't know what to expect from these new kinds of cows."

The lady from Philadelphia asked where the milk was kept.

"In the new dairy," answered Elizabeth Eliza.

"Is that in a cool place?" asked the lady from Philadelphia.

Elizabeth Eliza explained it was close by the new kitchen.

"Is it near the chimney?" inquired the lady from Philadelphia.

"It is directly back of the chimney and the new kitchen range," replied Elizabeth Eliza. "I suppose it is too hot!"

"Well, well!" said Mrs. Peterkin, "that is it! Last winter the milk froze, and now we have gone to the other extreme! Where shall we put our dairy?"

THE PETERKINS' CHRISTMAS-TREE.

———◆———

ARLY in the autumn the Peterkins began to prepare for their Christmas-tree. Everything was done in great privacy, as it was to be a surprise to the neighbors, as well as to the rest of the family. Mr. Peterkin had been up to Mr. Bromwick's wood-lot, and, with his consent, selected the tree. Agamemnon went to look at it occasionally after dark, and Solomon John made frequent visits to it mornings, just after sunrise. Mr. Peterkin drove Elizabeth Eliza and her mother that way, and pointed furtively to it with his whip; but none of them ever spoke of it aloud to each other. It was suspected that the little boys had been to see it Wednesday and Saturday afternoons. But they came home with their pockets full of chestnuts, and said nothing about it.

At length Mr. Peterkin had it cut down and brought secretly into the Larkins' barn.

A week or two before Christmas a measurement was made of it with Elizabeth Eliza's yard-measure. To Mr. Peterkin's great dismay it was discovered that it was too high to stand in the back parlor.

This fact was brought out at a secret council of Mr. and Mrs. Peterkin, Elizabeth Eliza, and Agamemnon.

Agamemnon suggested that it might be set up slanting; but Mrs. Peterkin was very sure it would make her dizzy, and the candles would drip.

But a brilliant idea came to Mr. Peterkin. He proposed that the ceiling of the parlor should be raised to make room for the top of the tree.

Elizabeth Eliza thought the space would need to be quite large. It must not be like a small box, or you could not see the tree.

"Yes," said Mr. Peterkin, "I should have the ceiling lifted all across the room; the effect would be finer."

Elizabeth Eliza objected to having the whole ceiling raised, because her room was over the back parlor, and she would have no floor while the alteration was going on, which would be very awkward. Besides, her room

was not very high now, and, if the floor were raised, perhaps she could not walk in it upright.

Mr. Peterkin explained that he didn't propose altering
the whole ceiling, but to lift up a ridge across the room
at the back part where the tree was to stand. This would
make a hump, to be sure, in Elizabeth Eliza's room; but
it would go across the whole room.

Elizabeth Eliza said she would not mind that. It
would be like the cuddy thing that comes up on the deck
of a ship, that you sit against, only here you would not
have the sea-sickness. She thought she should like it, for
a rarity. She might use it for a divan.

Mrs. Peterkin thought it would come in the worn
place of the carpet, and might be a convenience in making
the carpet over.

Agamemnon was afraid there would be trouble in
keeping the matter secret, for it would be a long piece of
work for a carpenter; but Mr. Peterkin proposed having
the carpenter for a day or two, for a number of other jobs

One of them was to make all
the chairs in the house of the same
height, for Mrs. Peterkin had nearly
broken her spine by sitting down in
a chair that she had supposed was
her own rocking-chair, and it had
proved to be two inches lower. The
little boys were now large enough

to sit in any chair; so a medium was fixed upon to satisfy

all the family, and the chairs were made uniformly of the same height.

On consulting the carpenter, however, he insisted that the tree could be cut off at the lower end to suit the height of the parlor, and demurred at so great a change as altering the ceiling. But Mr. Peterkin had set his mind upon the improvement, and Elizabeth Eliza had cut her carpet in preparation for it.

So the folding-doors into the back parlor were closed, and for nearly a fortnight before Christmas there was  great litter of fallen plastering, and laths, and chips, and shavings; and Elizabeth Eliza's carpet was taken up, and the furniture had to be changed, and one night she had to sleep at the Bromwicks', for there was a long hole in her floor that might be dangerous.

All this delighted the little boys. They could not understand what was going on. Perhaps they suspected a Christmas-tree, but they did not know why a Christmas-tree should have so many chips, and were still more astonished at the hump that appeared in Elizabeth Eliza's room. It must be a Christmas present, or else the tree in a box.

Some aunts and uncles, too, arrived a day or two before Christmas, with some small cousins. These cousins occupied the attention of the little boys, and there was a great deal of whispering and mystery, behind doors, and under the stairs. and in the corners of the entry.

Solomon John was busy, privately making some candles for the tree. He had been collecting some bayberries, as he understood they made very nice candles, so that it would not be necessary to buy any.

The elders of the family never all went into the back parlor together, and all tried not to see what was going on. Mrs. Peterkin would go in with Solomon John, or Mr. Peterkin with Elizabeth Eliza, or Elizabeth Eliza and Agamemnon and Solomon John. The little boys and the small cousins were never allowed even to look inside the room.

Elizabeth Eliza meanwhile went into town a number of times. She wanted to consult Amanda as to how much ice-cream they should need, and whether they could make it at home, as they had cream and ice. She was pretty busy in her own room; the furniture had to be changed, and the carpet altered. The "hump" was higher than she expected. There was danger of bumping her own head whenever she crossed it. She had to nail some padding on the ceiling for fear of accidents.

The afternoon before Christmas, Elizabeth Eliza, Solomon John, and their father collected in the back parlor for a council. The carpenters had done their work, and the tree stood at its full height at the back of the room, the top stretching up into the space arranged for it. All 'he chips and shavings were cleared away, and it stood on a neat box.

But what were they to put upon the tree?

Solomon John had brought in his supply of candles; but they proved to be very "stringy" and very few of

them. It was strange how many bayberries it took to make a few candles! The little boys had helped him, and he had gathered as much as a bushel of bayberries. He had put them in water, and skimmed off the wax, according to the directions; but there was so little wax!

Solomon John had given the little boys some of the bits sawed off from the legs of the chairs. He had suggested that they should cover them with gilt paper, to answer for gilt apples, without telling them what they were for.

These apples, a little blunt at the end, and the candles, were all they had for the tree!

After all her trips into town Elizabeth Eliza had forgotten to bring anything for it.

"I thought of candies and sugar-plums," she said; "but I concluded if we made caramels ourselves we should not need them. But, then, we have not made caramels. The fact is, that day my head was full of my carpet. I had bumped it pretty badly, too."

Mr. Peterkin wished he had taken, instead of a fir-tree, an apple-tree he had seen in October, full of red fruit.

"But the leaves would have fallen off by this time," said Elizabeth Eliza.

"And the apples, too," said Solomon John.

"It is odd I should have forgotten, that day I went in on purpose to get the things," said Elizabeth Eliza, musingly. "But I went from shop to shop, and didn't know exactly what to get. I saw a great many gilt things for Christmas-trees; but I knew the little boys were making the gilt apples; there were plenty of candles in the shops, but I knew Solomon John was making the candles."

Mr. Peterkin thought it was quite natural.

Solomon John wondered if it were too late for them to go into town now.

Elizabeth Eliza could not go in the next morning, for there was to be a grand Christmas dinner, and Mr. Peterkin could not be spared, and Solomon John was sure he and Agamemnon would not know what to buy. Besides, they would want to try the candles to-night.

Mr. Peterkin asked if the presents everybody had been preparing would not answer. But Elizabeth Eliza knew they would be too heavy.

A gloom came over the room. There was only a flickering gleam from one of Solomon John's candles that he had lighted by way of trial.

Solomon John again proposed going into town. He lighted a match to examine the newspaper about the trains. There were plenty of trains coming out at that hour, but none going in except a very late one. That would not leave time to do anything and come back.

"We could go in, Elizabeth Eliza and I," said Solomon John, "but we should not have time to buy anything."

Agamemnon was summoned in. Mrs. Peterkin was entertaining the uncles and aunts in the front parlor. Agamemnon wished there was time to study up something about electric lights. If they could only have a calcium light! Solomon John's candle sputtered and went out.

At this moment there was a loud knocking at the front door. The little boys, and the small cousins, and the uncles and aunts, and Mrs. Peterkin, hastened to see what was the matter.

The uncles and aunts thought somebody's house must be on fire. The door was opened, and there was a man, white with flakes, for it was beginning to snow, and he was pulling in a large box.

Mrs. Peterkin supposed it contained some of Elizabeth Eliza's purchases, so she ordered it to be pushed into the back parlor, and hastily called back her guests and the little boys into the other room. The little boys and the small cousins were sure they had seen Santa Claus himself.

Mr. Peterkin lighted the gas. The box was addressed to Elizabeth Eliza. It was from the lady from

Philadelphia! She had gathered a hint from Elizabeth
Eliza's letters that there was to be a Christmas-tree, and
had filled this box with all that would be needed.

It was opened directly. There was every kind of
gilt hanging-thing, from gilt pea-pods to butterflies on
springs. There were shining flags and lanterns, and bird-
cages, and nests with birds sitting on them, baskets of
fruit, gilt apples and bunches of grapes, and, at the
bottom of the whole, a large box of candles and a box
of Philadelphia bonbons!

Elizabeth Eliza and Solomon John could scarcely
keep from screaming. The little boys and the small
cousins knocked on
the folding-doors to
ask what was the
matter.

Hastily Mr.
Peterkin and the
rest took out the things and hung them on the tree,
and put on the candles.

When all was done, it looked so well that Mr.
Peterkin exclaimed:—

"Let us light the candles now, and send to invite
all the neighbors to-night, and have the tree on Christmas Eve!"

And so it was that the Peterkins had their Christmas-tree the day before, and on Christmas night could
go and visit their neighbors.

MRS. PETERKIN'S TEA-PARTY.

T WAS important to have a tea-party, as they had all been invited by everybody, — the Bromwicks, the Tremletts, and the Gibbonses. It would be such a good chance to pay off some of their old debts, now that the lady from Philadelphia was back again, and her two daughters, who would be sure to make it all go off well.

But as soon as they began to make out the list they saw there were too many to have at once, for there were but twelve cups and saucers in the best set.

"There are seven of *us*, to begin with," said Mr. Peterkin.

"We need not all drink tea," said Mrs. Peterkin.

"I never do," said Solomon John. The little boys never did.

"And we could have coffee, too," suggested Eliza-beth Eliza.

"That would take as many cups," objected Aga-memnon.

"We could use the every-day set for the coffee,"

answered Elizabeth Eliza; "they are the right shape.
Besides," she went on, "they would not all come. Mr.
and Mrs. Bromwick, for instance; they never go out."

"There are but
six cups in the every-
day set," said Mrs.
Peterkin.

The little boys
said there were plenty
of saucers; and Mr.

Peterkin agreed with Elizabeth Eliza that all would not
come. Old Mr. Jeffers never went out.

"There are three of the Tremletts," said Elizabeth
Eliza; "they never go out together. One of them, if not
two, will be sure to have the headache. Ann Maria
Bromwick would come, and the three Gibbons boys, and
their sister Juliana; but the other sisters are out West,
and there is but one Osborne."

It really did seem safe to ask "everybody." They
would be sorry, after it was over, that they had not
asked more.

"We have the cow," said Mrs. Peterkin, "so there
will be as much cream and milk as we shall need."

"And our own pig," said Agamemnon. "I am glad
we had it salted; so we can have plenty of sandwiches."

"I will buy a chest of tea," exclaimed Mr. Peterkin,
"I have been thinking of a chest for some time."

Mrs. Peterkin thought a whole chest would not be needed; it was as well to buy the tea and coffee by the pound. But Mr. Peterkin determined on a chest of tea and a bag of coffee.

So they decided to give the invitations to all. It might be a stormy evening, and some would be prevented.

The lady from Philadelphia and her daughters accepted.

And it turned out a fair day, and more came than were expected. Ann Maria Bromwick had a friend staying with her, and brought her over, for the Bromwicks were opposite neighbors. And the Tremletts had a niece, and Mary Osborne an aunt, that they took the liberty to bring.

The little boys were at the door, to show in the guests, and as each set came to the front gate they ran back to tell their mother that more were coming. Mrs. Peterkin had grown dizzy with counting those who had come, and trying to calculate how many were to come, and wondering why there were always more and never less, and whether the cups would go round.

The three Tremletts all came, with their niece. They all had had their headaches the day before, and were having that banged feeling you always have after a headache; so they all sat at the same side of the room on the long sofa.

All the Jefferses came, though they had sent uncertain answers. Old Mr. Jeffers had to be helped in, with his cane, by Mr. Peterkin.

The Gibbons boys came, and would stand just outside the parlor door. And Juliana appeared afterward, with the two other sisters, unexpectedly home from the West.

"Got home this morning!" they said. "And so glad to be in time to see everybody, — a little tired, to be sure, after forty-eight hours in a sleeping-car!"

"Forty-eight!" repeated Mrs. Peterkin; and wondered if there were forty-eight people, and why they were all so glad to come, and whether all could sit down.

Old Mr. and Mrs. Bromwick came. They thought it would not be neighborly to stay away. They insisted on getting into the most uncomfortable seats.

Yet there seemed to be seats enough while the Gibbons boys preferred to stand. But they never could sit round a tea-table. Elizabeth Eliza had thought they all might have room at the table, and Solomon John and the little boys could help in the waiting.

It was a great moment when the lady from Philadelphia arrived with her daughters. Mr. Peterkin was talking to Mr. Bromwick, who was a little deaf. The Gibbons boys retreated a little farther behind the parlor door. Mrs. Peterkin hastened forward to shake hands with the lady from Philadelphia, saying · —

"Four Gibbons girls and Mary Osborne's aunt,— that makes nineteen; and now"—

It made no difference what she said; for there was such a murmuring of talk that any words suited. And the lady from Philadelphia wanted to be introduced to the Bromwicks.

It was delightful for the little boys. They came to Elizabeth Eliza, and asked:—

"Can't we go and ask more?   Can't we fetch the Larkins ?"

"Oh, dear, no!" answered Elizabeth Eliza. "I can't even count them."

Mrs. Peterkin found time to meet Elizabeth Eliza in the side entry, to ask if there were going to be cups enough.

"I have set Agamemnon in the front entry to count," said Elizabeth Eliza, putting her hand to her head.

The little boys came to say that the Maberlys were coming.

"The Maberlys!" exclaimed Elizabeth Eliza. "I never asked them."

"It is your father's doing," cried Mrs. Peterkin. "I do believe he asked everybody he saw!" And she hurried back to her guests.

"What if father really has asked everybody?" Elizabeth Eliza said to herself, pressing her head again with her hand.

There were the cow and the pig. But if they all took tea or coffee, or both, the cups could *not* go round.

Agamemnon returned in the midst of her agony.

He had not been able to count the guests, they moved about so, they talked so; and it would not look well to appear to count.

"What shall we do?" exclaimed Elizabeth Eliza.

"We are not a family for an emergency," said Aga-memnon.

"What do you suppose they did in Philadelphia at the Exhibition, when there were more people than cups and saucers?" asked Elizabeth Eliza. "Could not you go and inquire? I know the lady from Philadelphia is talking about the Exhibition, and telling how she stayed at home to receive friends. And they must have had trouble there! Could not you go in and ask, just as if you wanted to know?"

Agamemnon looked into the room, but there were too many talking with the lady from Philadelphia.

"If we could only look into some book," he said, — "the encyclopædia or the dictionary; they are such a help sometimes!"

At this moment he thought of his "Great Triumphs of Great Men," that he was reading just now. He had not reached the lives of the Stephensons, or any of the men of modern times. He might skip over to them, — he knew they were men for emergencies.

He ran up to his room, and met Solomon John coming down with chairs.

"That is a good thought," said Agamemnon. "I will bring down more upstairs chairs."

"No," said Solomon John. "here are all that can come

down; the rest of the bedroom chairs match bureaus, and they never will do! "

Agamemnon kept on to his own room, to consult his books. If only he could invent something on the spur of the moment, — a set of bedroom furniture, that in an emergency could be turned into parlor chairs! It seemed an idea; and he sat himself down to his table and pencils, when he was interrupted by the little boys, who came to tell him that Elizabeth Eliza wanted him.

The little boys had been busy thinking. They proposed that the tea-table, with all the things on, should be pushed into the front room, where the company were; and those could take cups who could find cups.

But Elizabeth Eliza feared it would not be safe to push so large a table; it might upset, and break what china they had.

Agamemnon came down to find her pouring out tea, in the back room. She called to him: —

"Agamemnon, you must bring Mary Osborne to help, and perhaps one of the Gibbons boys would carry round some of the cups."

And so she began to pour out, and to send round the sandwiches, and the tea, and the coffee. Let things go as far as they would!

The little boys took the sugar and cream.

"As soon as they have done drinking bring back the cups and saucers to be washed," she said to the Gibbons boys and the little boys.

This was an idea of Mary Osborne's.

But what was their surprise that the more they poured out the more cups they seemed to have! Elizabeth Eliza took the coffee, and Mary Osborne the tea. Amanda brought fresh cups from the kitchen.

"I can't understand it," Elizabeth Eliza said to Amanda. "Do they come back to you round through the piazza? Surely there are more cups than there were!"

Her surprise was greater when some of them proved to be coffee-cups that matched the set! And they never had had coffee-cups.

Solomon John came in at this moment, breathless with triumph.

"Solomon John!" Elizabeth Eliza exclaimed; "I cannot understand the cups!"

"It is my doing," said Solomon John, with an elevated air. "I went to the lady from Philadelphia, in the midst of her talk. 'What do you do in Philadelphia, when you haven't enough cups?' 'Borrow of my neighbors,' she answered, as quick as she could."

"She must have guessed," interrupted Elizabeth Eliza.

"That may be," said Solomon John. "But I whispered to Ann Maria Bromwick, — she was standing by, — and she took me straight over into their closet, and old Mr. Bromwick bought this set just where we bought ours. And they had a coffee-set, too" —

"You mean where our father and mother bought them. We were not born," said Elizabeth Eliza.

"It is all the same," said Solomon John. "They match exactly."

So they did, and more and more came in.

Elizabeth Eliza exclaimed: —

"And Agamemnon says we are not a family for emergencies!"

"Ann Maria was very good about it," said Solomon John; "and quick, too. And old Mrs. Bromwick has kept all her set of two dozen coffee and tea cups!"

Elizabeth Eliza was ready to faint with delight and relief. She told the Gibbons boys, by mistake, instead of Agamemnon and the little boys. She almost let fall the cups and saucers she took in her hand.

"No trouble now!"

She thought of the cow, and she thought of the pig, and she poured on.

No trouble, except about the chairs. She looked into the room; all seemed to be sitting down, even her mother No, her father was standing, talking to Mr. Jeffers. But he was drinking coffee, and the Gibbons boys were handing things around.

The daughters of the lady from Philadelphia were sitting on shawls on the edge of the window that opened upon the piazza. It was a soft, warm evening, and some of the young people were on the piazza. Everybody was talking and laughing, except those who were listening.

Mr. Peterkin broke away, to bring back his cup and another for more coffee.

"It's a great success, Elizabeth Eliza," he whispered. "The coffee is admirable, and plenty of cups. We asked none too many. I should not mind having a tea-party every week."

Elizabeth Eliza sighed with relief as she filled his cup. It was going off well. There were cups enough, but she was not sure she could live over another such hour of anxiety; and what was to be done after tea?

THE PETERKINS TOO LATE FOR THE EXHIBITION

———•———

Dramatis Personæ. — Amanda (friend of Elizabeth Eliza), Amanda's mother, girls of the graduating class, Mrs. Peterkin, Elizabeth Eliza.

AMANDA [*coming in with a few graduates*].

MOTHER, the exhibition is over, and I have brought the whole class home to the collation.

MOTHER. — The whole class! But I only expected a few.

AMANDA. — The rest are coming. I brought Julie, and Clara, and Sophie with me. [*A voice is heard.*] Here are the rest.

MOTHER. — Why, no. It is Mrs. Peterkin and Elizabeth Eliza!

AMANDA. — Too late for the exhibition. Such a shame! But in time for the collation.

MOTHER [*to herself*]. — If the ice-cream will go round.

AMANDA. — But what made you so late? Did you miss the train? This is Elizabeth Eliza, girls, — you have heard me speak of her. What a pity you were too late.

MRS. PETERKIN. — We tried to come; we did our best.

MOTHER. — Did you miss the train? Didn't you get my postal-card?

MRS. PETERKIN. — We had nothing to do with the train.

AMANDA. — You don't mean you walked?

MRS. PETERKIN. — Oh, no, indeed!

ELIZABETH ELIZA. — We came in a horse and carry-all.

JULIA. — I always wondered how anybody could come in a horse!

AMANDA. — You are too foolish, Julie. They came in the carryall part. But didn't you start in time?

MRS. PETERKIN. — It all comes from the carryall being so hard to turn. I told Mr. Peterkin we should get into trouble with one of those carryalls that don't turn easy.

ELIZABETH ELIZA. — They turn easy enough in the stable, so you can't tell.

MRS. PETERKIN. — Yes; we started with the little boys and Solomon John on the back seat, and Elizabeth Eliza on the front. She was to drive, and I was to see to the driving. But the horse was not faced toward Boston.

MOTHER. — And you tipped over in turning round! Oh, what an accident!

AMANDA. — And the little boys, — where are they? Are they killed?

ELIZABETH ELIZA. — The little boys are all safe. We left them at the Pringles', with Solomon John.

MOTHER. — But what did happen?

MRS. PETERKIN. — We started the wrong way.

MOTHER. — You lost your way, after all?

ELIZABETH ELIZA. — No; we knew the way well enough.

AMANDA. — It's as plain as a pikestaff!

MRS. PETERKIN. — No; we had the horse faced in the wrong direction, — toward Providence.

ELIZABETH ELIZA. — And mother was afraid to have me turn, and we kept on and on till we should reach a wide place.

MRS. PETERKIN. — I thought we should come to a road that would veer off to the right or left, and bring us back to the right direction.

MOTHER. — Could not you all get out and turn the thing round?

MRS. PETERKIN. — Why, no; if it had broken down we should not have been in anything, and could not have gone anywhere.

ELIZABETH ELIZA. — Yes, I have always heard it was best to stay in the carriage, whatever happens.

JULIA. — But nothing seemed to happen.

MRS. PETERKIN. — Oh, yes; we met one man after another, and we asked the way to Boston.

ELIZABETH ELIZA. — And all they would say was, "Turn right round, — you are on the road to Providence."

MRS. PETERKIN. — As if we could turn right round! That was just what we couldn't.

MOTHER. — You don't mean you kept on all the way to Providence?

ELIZABETH ELIZA. — Oh, dear, no! We kept on and on, till we met a man with a black hand-bag, — black leather, I should say.

JULIA. — He must have been a book-agent.

MRS. PETERKIN. — I dare say he was; his bag seemed heavy. He set it on a stone.

MOTHER. — I dare say it was the same one that came here the other day. He wanted me to buy the "History of the Aborigines, Brought up from Earliest Times to the Present Date," in four volumes. I told him I hadn't time to read so much. He said that was no matter, few did, and it wasn't much worth it; they bought books for the look of the thing.

AMANDA. — Now, that was illiterate; he never could have graduated. I hope, Elizabeth Eliza, you had nothing to do with that man.

ELIZABETH ELIZA. — Very likely it was not the same one.

MOTHER. — Did he have a kind of pepper-and-salt suit with one of the buttons worn?

MRS. PETERKIN. — I noticed one of the buttons was off.

AMANDA. — We're off the subject. Did you buy his book?

ELIZABETH ELIZA. — He never offered us his book.

MRS. PETERKIN. — He told us the same story, — we were going to Providence ; if we wanted to go to Boston we must turn directly round.

ELIZABETH ELIZA. — I told him I couldn't; but he took the horse's head, and the first thing I knew —

AMANDA. — He had yanked you round!

MRS. PETERKIN. — I screamed; I couldn't help it!

ELIZABETH ELIZA. — I was glad when it was over!

MOTHER. — Well, well; it shows the disadvantage of starting wrong.

MRS. PETERKIN. — Yes, we came straight enough when the horse was headed right; but we lost time.

ELIZABETH ELIZA. — I am sorry enough I lost the exhibition, and seeing you take the diploma, Amanda. I never got the diploma myself. I came near it.

MRS. PETERKIN. — Somehow, Elizabeth Eliza never succeeded. I think there was partiality about the promotions.

ELIZABETH ELIZA. — I never was good about remembering things. I studied well enough, but when I came to say off my lesson I couldn't think what it was. Yet I could have answered some of the other girls' questions.

JULIA. — It's odd how the other girls always have the easiest questions.

ELIZABETH ELIZA. — I never could remember poetry. There was only one thing I could repeat.

AMANDA. — Oh, do let us have it now; and then we'll recite to you some of our exhibition pieces.

ELIZABETH ELIZA. — I'll try.

MRS. PETERKIN. — Yes, Elizabeth Eliza, do what you can to help entertain Amanda's friends.

[*All stand looking at* ELIZABETH ELIZA, *who remains silent and thoughtful.*]

ELIZABETH ELIZA. — I'm trying to think what it is about. You all know it. You remember, Amanda, — the name is rather long.

AMANDA. — It can't be Nebuchadnezzar, can it? —that is one of the longest names I know.

ELIZABETH ELIZA. Oh, dear, no!

JULIA. —Perhaps it's Cleopatra.

ELIZABETH ELIZA. — It does begin with a "C," — only he was a boy.

AMANDA. — That's a pity, for it might be "We are seven," only that is a girl. Some of them were boys.

ELIZABETH ELIZA. — It begins about a boy — if I could only think where he was. I can't remember.

AMANDA. — Perhaps he "stood upon the burning deck"?

ELIZABETH ELIZA. —That's just it; I knew he stood somewhere.

AMANDA. — Casabianca! Now begin — go ahead.

ELIZABETH ELIZA. —

"The boy stood on the burning deck,
    When — when" —

I can't think who stood there with him.

JULIA. — If the deck was burning, it must have been on fire. I guess the rest ran away, or jumped into boats.

AMANDA. — That's just it: —

"Whence all but him had fled."

ELIZABETH ELIZA. — I think I can say it now.

"The boy stood on the burning deck,
    Whence all but him had fled" —

[*She hesitates.*] Then I think he went —

JULIA. — Of course, he fled after the rest.

AMANDA. — Dear, no! That's the point. He didn't.

"The flames rolled on, he would not go
    Without his father's word."

ELIZABETH ELIZA. — Oh, yes. Now I can say it.

"The boy stood on the burning deck,
    Whence all but him had fled;
The flames rolled on, he would not go
    Without his father's word."

But it used to rhyme. I don't know what has happened to it.

Mrs. Peterkin. — Elizabeth Eliza is very particular about the rhymes.

Elizabeth Eliza. — It must be "without his father's *head*," or, perhaps, "without his father *said*" he should.

Julia. — I think you must have omitted something.

Amanda. — She has left out ever so much!

Mother. — Perhaps it's as well to omit some, for the ice-cream has come, and you must all come down.

Amanda. — And here are the rest of the girls; and let us all unite in a song!

[*Exeunt omnes singing.*]

THE PETERKINS CELEBRATE THE FOURTH OF JULY.

T HE day began early.

A compact had been made with the little boys the evening before.

They were to be allowed to usher in the glorious day by the blowing of horns exactly at sunrise. But they were to blow them for precisely five minutes only, and no sound of the horns should be heard afterward till the family were downstairs.

It was thought that a peace might thus be bought by a short, though crowded, period of noise.

The morning came. Even before the morning, at half-past three o'clock, a terrible blast of the horns aroused the whole family.

Mrs. Peterkin clasped her hands to her head and exclaimed: "I am thankful the lady from Philadelphia is not here!" For she had been invited to stay a week, but had declined to come before the Fourth of July, as she was not well, and her doctor had prescribed quiet.

And the number of the horns was most remarkable! It was as though every cow in the place had arisen and was blowing through both her own horns!

"How many little boys are there? How many have we?" exclaimed Mr. Peterkin, going over their names one by one mechanically, thinking he would do it, as he might count imaginary sheep jumping over a fence, to put himself to sleep. Alas! the counting could not put him to sleep now, in such a din.

And how unexpectedly long the five minutes seemed! Elizabeth Eliza was to take out her watch and give the signal for the end of the five minutes, and the ceasing of the horns. Why did not the signal come? Why did not Elizabeth Eliza stop them?

And certainly it was long before sunrise; there was no dawn to be seen!

"We will not try this plan again," said Mrs. Peterkin.

"If we live to another Fourth," added Mr. Peterkin, hastening to the door to inquire into the state of affairs.

Alas! Amanda, by mistake, had waked up the little boys an hour too early. And by another mistake the little boys had invited three or four of their friends to spend the night with them. Mrs. Peterkin had given them permission to have the boys for the whole day, and they understood the day as beginning when they went to bed the night before. This accounted for the number of horns

It would have been impossible to hear any explana‑
tion; but the five minutes were over, and the horns had

ceased, and there remained only
the noise of a singular leaping
of feet, explained perhaps by
a possible pillow-fight, that kept
the family below partially awake
until the bells and cannon made
known the dawning of the glorious day, — the sunrise, or
"the rising of the sons," as Mr. Peterkin jocosely called
it when they heard the little boys and their friends clat‑
tering down the stairs to begin the outside festivities.

They were bound first for the swamp, for Elizabeth
Eliza, at the suggestion of the lady from Philadelphia,
had advised them to hang some flags around the pillars
of the piazza. Now the little boys knew of a place in
the swamp where they had been in the habit of digging
for "flag-root," and where they might find plenty of flag
flowers. They did bring away all they could, but they
were a little out of bloom. The boys were in the midst
of nailing up all they had on the pillars of the piazza,
when the procession of the Antiques and Horribles passed
along. As the procession saw the festive arrangements
on the piazza, and the crowd of boys, who cheered them
loudly, it stopped to salute the house with some especial
strains of greeting.

Poor Mrs. Peterkin! They were directly under her
windows! In a few moments of quiet, during the boys'

absence from the house on their visit to the swamp, she had been trying to find out whether she had a sick-head-ache, or whether it was all the noise, and she was just deciding it was the sick headache, but was falling into a light slumber, when the fresh noise outside began.

There were the imitations of the crowing of cocks, and braying of donkeys, and the sound of horns, encored and increased by the cheers of the boys. Then began the torpedoes, and the Antiques and Horribles had Chinese crackers also.

And, in despair of sleep, the family came down to breakfast.

Mrs. Peterkin had always been much afraid of fire-works, and had never allowed the boys to bring gun-powder into the house. She was even afraid of torpedoes; they looked so much like sugar-plums she was sure some of the children would swallow them, and explode before anybody knew it.

She was very timid about other things. She was not sure even about pea-nuts. Everybody exclaimed over this: "Surely there was no danger in pea-nuts!" But Mrs. Peterkin declared she had been very much alarmed at the Centennial Exhibition, and in the crowded corners of the streets in Boston, at the pea-nut stands, where they had machines to roast the pea-nuts. She did not think it was safe. They might go off any time, in the midst of a crowd of people, too!

Mr. Peterkin thought there actually was no danger,

and he should be sorry to give up the pea-nut. He thought it an American institution, something really belonging to the Fourth of July. He even confessed to a quiet pleasure in crushing the empty shells with his feet on the sidewalks as he went along the streets.

Agamemnon thought it a simple joy.

In consideration, however, of the fact that they had had no real celebration of the Fourth the last year, Mrs. Peterkin had consented to give over the day, this year, to the amusement of the family as a Centennial celebration. She would prepare herself for a terrible noise, — only she did not want any gunpowder brought into the house.

The little boys had begun by firing some torpedoes a few days beforehand, that their mother might be used to the sound, and had selected their horns some weeks before.

Solomon John had been very busy in inventing some fireworks. As Mrs. Peterkin objected to the use of gunpowder, he found out from the dictionary what the different parts of gunpowder are, — saltpetre, charcoal, and sulphur. Charcoal, he discovered, they had in the wood-house; saltpetre they would find in the cellar, in the beef barrel; and sulphur they could buy at the apothecary's. He explained to his mother that these materials had never yet exploded in the house, and she was quieted.

Agamemnon, meanwhile, remembered a recipe he had

read somewhere for making a "fulminating paste" of iron-filings and powder of brimstone. He had written it down on a piece of paper in his pocket-book. But the iron filings must be finely powdered. This they began upon a day or two before, and the very afternoon before laid out some of the paste on the piazza.

Pin-wheels and rockets were contributed by Mr. Peterkin for the evening. According to a programme drawn up by Agamemnon and Solomon John, the reading of the Declaration of Independence was to take place in the morning, on the piazza, under the flags.

The Bromwicks brought over their flag to hang over the door.

"That is what the lady from Philadelphia meant," explained Elizabeth Eliza.

"She said the flags of our country," said the little boys. "We thought she meant 'in the country.'"

Quite a company assembled; but it seemed nobody had a copy of the Declaration of Independence.

Elizabeth Eliza said she could say one line, if they each could add as much. But it proved they all knew the same line that she did, as they began : —

"When, in the course of — when, in the course of —

when, in the course of human — when in the course of human events — when, in the course of human events, it becomes — when, in the course of human events, it becomes necessary — when, in the course of human events, it becomes necessary for one people" —

They could not get any farther. Some of the party decided that "one people" was a good place to stop, and the little boys sent off some fresh torpedoes in honor of the people. But Mr. Peterkin was not satisfied. He invited the assembled party to stay until sunset, and meanwhile he would find a copy, and torpedoes were to be saved to be fired off at the close of every sentence.

And now the noon bells rang and the noon bells ceased.

Mrs. Peterkin wanted to ask everybody to dinner. She should have some cold beef. She had let Amanda go, because it was the Fourth, and everybody ought to be free that one day; so she could not have much of a dinner. But when she went to cut her beef she found Solomon had taken it to soak, on account of the saltpetre, for the fireworks!

Well, they had a pig; so she took a ham, and the boys had bought tamarinds and buns and a cocoa-nut. So the company stayed on, and when the Antiques and Horribles passed again they were treated to pea-nuts and lemonade.

They sung patriotic songs, they told stories, they fired torpedoes, they frightened the cats with them. It was a warm afternoon; the red poppies were out wide, and the hot sun poured down on the alley-ways in the garden. There was a seething sound of a hot day in the buzzing of insects, in the steaming heat that came up from the ground. Some neighboring boys were firing a toy cannon. Every time it went off Mrs. Peterkin started, and looked to see if one of the little boys was gone. Mr. Peterkin had set out to find a copy of the "Declaration." Agamemnon had disappeared. She had not a moment to decide about her headache. She asked Ann Maria if she were not anxious about the fireworks, and if rockets were not dangerous.

They went up, but you were never sure where they came down.

And then came a fresh tumult! All the fire-engines in town rushed toward them, clanging with bells, men and boys yelling! They were out for a practice, and for a Fourth-of-July show.

Mrs. Peterkin thought the house was on fire, and so did some of the guests. There was great rushing hither and thither. Some thought they would better go home; some thought they would better stay. Mrs. Peterkin hastened into the house to save herself, or see what she could save. Elizabeth Eliza followed her, first proceeding to collect all the pokers and tongs she could find, because they could be thrown out of the window without breaking. She had read of people who had flung looking-glasses out of the window by mistake, in the excitement of the house being on fire, and had carried the pokers and tongs carefully into the garden. There was nothing like being prepared. She had always determined to do the reverse. So with calmness she told Solomon John to take down the looking-glasses. But she met with a difficulty,—there were no pokers and tongs, as they did not use them. They had no open fires; Mrs. Peterkin had been afraid of them.

So Elizabeth Eliza took all the pots and kettles up to the upper windows, ready to be thrown out.

But where was Mrs. Peterkin? Solomon John found she had fled to the attic in terror. He persuaded her to come down, assuring her it was the most unsafe place; but she in-

sisted upon stopping to collect some bags of old pieces, that nobody would think of saving from the general wreck, she said, unless she did. Alas! this was the result of fireworks on Fourth of July! As they came downstairs they heard the voices of all the company declaring there was no fire; the danger was past. It was long before Mrs. Peterkin could believe it. They told her the fire company was only out for show,  and to celebrate the Fourth of July. She thought it already too much celebrated.

Elizabeth Eliza's kettles and pans had come down through the windows with a crash, that had only added to the festivities, the little boys thought.

Mr. Peterkin had been roaming about all this time in search of a copy of the Declaration of Independence. The public library was shut, and he had to go from  house to house; but now, as the sunset bells and cannon began, he returned with a copy, and read it, to the pealing of the bells and sounding of the cannon. Torpedoes and crackers were fired at every pause. Some sweet-marjoram pots, tin cans filled with crackers which were lighted, went off with great explosions.

At the most exciting moment, near the close of the reading, Agamemnon, with an expression of terror, pulled Solomon John aside.

"I have suddenly remembered where I read about the 'fulminating paste' we made. It was in the preface to 'Woodstock,' and I have been round to borrow the book, to read the directions over again, because I was afraid about the 'paste' going off. READ THIS QUICKLY! and tell me, *Where is the fulminating paste?*"

Solomon John was busy winding some covers of paper over a little parcel. It contained chlorate of potash and sulphur mixed. A friend had told him of the composition. The more thicknesses of paper you put round it the louder it would go off. You must pound it with a hammer. Solomon John felt it must be perfectly safe, as his mother had taken potash for a medicine.

He still held the parcel as he read from Agamemnon's book: "This paste, when it has lain together about twenty-six hours, will *of itself* take fire, and burn all the sulphur away with a blue flame and a bad smell."

"Where is the paste?" repeated Solomon John, in terror.

"We made it just twenty-six hours ago," said Agamemnon.

"We put it on the piazza," exclaimed Solomon John, rapidly recalling the facts, "and it is in front of our mother's feet!"

He hastened to snatch the paste away before it should

take fire, flinging aside the packet in his hurry. Aga-
memnou, jumping upon the piazza at the same moment,
trod upon the paper parcel,
which exploded at once with
the shock, and he fell to the
ground, while at the same
moment the paste "fulmi-
nated" into a blue flame
directly in front of Mrs.
Peterkin!

It was a moment of great
confusion. There were cries and screams. The bells were
still ringing, the cannon firing, and Mr. Peterkin had just
reached the closing words: "Our lives, our fortunes, and
our sacred honor."

"We are all blown up, as I feared we should be,"
Mrs. Peterkin at length ventured to say, finding herself

in a lilac-bush by the side of the
piazza. She scarcely dared to open
her eyes to see the scattered limbs
about her.

It was so with all. Even Ann
Maria Bromwick clutched a pillar of
the piazza, with closed eyes.

At length Mr. Peterkin said,
calmly, "Is anybody killed?"

There was no reply. Nobody could tell whether it
was because everybody was killed, or because they were

too wounded to answer. It was a great while before Mrs.
Peterkin ventured to move.

But the little boys soon shouted with joy, and cheered
the success of Solomon John's fireworks, and hoped he
had some more. One of them had his face blackened by
an unexpected cracker, and Elizabeth Eliza's muslin dress
was burned here and there. But no one was hurt; no
one had lost any limbs, though Mrs. Peterkin was sure
she had seen some flying in the air. Nobody could understand how, as she had kept her eyes firmly shut.

No greater accident had occurred than
the singeing of the tip of Solomon John's
nose. But there was an unpleasant and
terrible odor from the "fulminating paste."

Mrs. Peterkin was extricated from the
lilac-bush. No one knew how she got there.
Indeed, the thundering noise had stunned
everybody. It had roused the neighborhood
even more than before. Answering explosions came on
every side, and, though the sunset light had not faded
away, the little boys hastened to send off rockets under
cover of the confusion. Solomon John's other fireworks
would not go. But all felt he had done enough.

Mrs. Peterkin retreated into the parlor, deciding she
really did have a headache. At times she had to come
out when a rocket went off, to see if it was one of the
little boys. She was exhausted by the adventures of the
day, and almost thought it could not have been worse if

AT LENGTH MR. PETERKIN SAID, CALMLY, "IS ANYBODY KILLED?"

the boys had been allowed gunpowder. The distracted lady was thankful there was likely to be but one Centennial Fourth in her lifetime, and declared she should never more keep anything in the house as dangerous as saltpetred beef, and she should never venture to take another spoonful of potash.

THE PETERKINS' PICNIC.

———◆———

HERE was some doubt about the weather. Solomon John looked at the "Probabilities"; there were to be "areas of rain" in the New England States.

Agamemnon thought if they could only know where the areas of rain were to be they might go to the others. Mr. Peterkin proposed walking round the house in a procession, to examine the sky. As they returned they met Ann Maria Bromwick, who was to go, much surprised not to find them ready.

Mr. and Mrs. Peterkin were to go in the carryall, and take up the lady from Philadelphia, and Ann Maria, with the rest, was to follow in a wagon, and to stop for the daughters of the lady from Philadelphia. The wagon arrived, and so Mr Peterkin had the horse put into the carryall.

A basket had been kept on the back piazza for some days, where anybody could put anything that would be needed for the picnic as soon as it was thought of. Agamemnon had already decided to take a thermometer; some-

body was always complaining of being too hot or too cold
at a picnic, and it would be a great convenience to see if she really were so. He thought
now he might take a barometer, as " Proba-
biiities" was so uncertain. Then, if it went
down in a threatening way, they could all
come back.

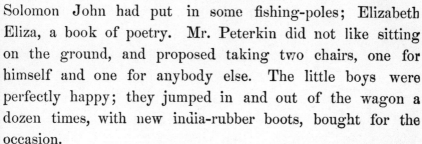

The little boys had tied their kites to
the basket. They had never tried them at
home; it might be a good chance on the hills.
Solomon John had put in some fishing-poles; Elizabeth
Eliza, a book of poetry. Mr. Peterkin did not like sitting
on the ground, and proposed taking two chairs, one for
himself and one for anybody else. The little boys were
perfectly happy; they jumped in and out of the wagon a
dozen times, with new india-rubber boots, bought for the
occasion.

Before they started, Mrs. Peterkin began to think she
had already had enough of the picnic,
what with going and coming, and trying
to remember things. So many mistakes
were made. The things that were to go
in the wagon were put in the carryall,
and the things in the carryall had to be
taken out for the wagon! Elizabeth
Eliza forgot her water-proof, and had to
go back for her veil, and Mr. Peterkin
came near forgetting his umbrella.

Mrs. Peterkin sat on the piazza and tried to think. She felt as if she must have forgotten something; she knew she must. Why could not she think of it now, before it was too late? It seems hard any day to think what to have for dinner, but how much easier now it would be to stay at home quietly and order the dinner,— and there was the butcher's cart! But now they must think of everything.

At last she was put into the carryall, and Mr. Peterkin in front to drive. Twice they started, and twice they found something was left behind,— the loaf of fresh brown

bread on the back piazza, and a basket of sandwiches on the front porch. And, just as the wagon was leaving, the little boys shrieked, "The basket of things was left behind!"

Everybody got out of the wagon. Agamemnon went back into the house, to see if anything else were left. He looked into the closets; he shut the front door, and was so busy that he forgot to get into the wagon himself. It started off and went down the street without him!

He was wondering what he should do if he were left behind (why had they not thought to arrange a telegraph wire to the back wheel of the wagon, so that he might have sent a message in such a case!), when the Bromwicks drove out of their yard, in their buggy, and took him in.

They joined the rest of the party at Tatham Corners where they were all to meet and consult where they were to go. Mrs. Peterkin called to Aga-memnon, as soon as he appeared. She had been holding the barometer and the thermometer, and they waggled so that it troubled her. It was hard keeping the thermometer out of the sun, which would make it so warm. It really took away her pleasure, holding the things. Agamemnon decided to get into the carryall, on the seat with his father, and take the barometer and thermometer.

The consultation went on. Should they go to Cherry Swamp, or Lonetown Hill? You had the view if you went to Lonetown Hill, but maybe the drive to Cherry Swamp was prettier.

Somebody suggested asking the lady from Philadelphia, as the picnic was got up for her.

But where was she?

"I declare," said Mr. Peterkin, "I forgot to stop for her!" The whole picnic there, and no lady from Philadelphia!

It seemed the horse had twitched his head in a threatening manner as they passed the house, and Mr.

Peterkin had forgotten to stop, and Mrs. Peterkin had been so busy managing the thermometers that she had not noticed, and the wagon had followed on behind.

Mrs. Peterkin was in despair. She knew they had forgotten something! She did not like to have Mr. Peterkin make a short turn, and it was getting late, and what  would the lady from Philadelphia think of it, and had they not better give it all up?

But everybody said "No!" and Mr. Peterkin said he could make a wide turn round the Lovejoy barn. So they made the turn, and took up the lady from Philadelphia, and the wagon followed behind and took up her daughters, for there was a driver in the wagon besides Solomon John.

Ann Maria Bromwick said it was so late by this time they might as well stop and have the picnic on the Common! But the question was put again, Where should they go?

The lady from Philadelphia decided for Strawberry Nook, — it sounded inviting. There were no strawberries, and there was no nook, it was said, but there was a good place to tie the horses.

Mrs. Peterkin was feeling a little nervous, for she did not know what the lady from Philadelphia would think of their having forgotten her, and the more she tried to explain it the worse it seemed to make it. She supposed they never did such things in Philadelphia; she knew they had invited all the world to a party, but she was sure she would never want to invite anybody again. There was no fun about it till it was all over. Such a mistake, — to have a party for a person, and then go without her; but she knew they would forget something! She wished they had not called it their picnic.

There was another bother! Mr. Peterkin stopped. "Was anything broke?" exclaimed Mrs. Peterkin. "Was something forgotten?" asked the lady from Philadelphia.

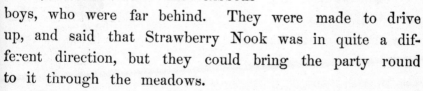

No! But Mr. Peterkin didn't know the way; and here he was leading all the party, and a long row of carriages following.

They all stopped, and it seemed nobody knew the way to Strawberry Nook, unless it was the Gibbons boys, who were far behind. They were made to drive up, and said that Strawberry Nook was in quite a different direction, but they could bring the party round to it through the meadows.

The lady from Philadelphia thought they might stop anywhere, such a pleasant day; but Mr. Peterkin said they were started for Strawberry Nook, and had better keep on.

So they kept on. It proved to be an excellent place, where they could tie the horses to a fence. Mrs. Peterkin did not like their all heading different ways; it seemed as if any of them might come at her, and tear up the fence, especially as the little boys had their kites flapping round. The Tremletts insisted upon the whole party going up on the hill; it was too damp below. So the Gibbons boys,

and the little boys, and Aga-memnon, and Solomon John, and all the party, had to carry everything up to the rocks. The large basket of " things " was very heavy. It had been difficult to lift it into the wagon, and it was harder to take it out. But, with the help of the driver, and Mr. Peter-kin, and old Mr. Bromwick, it was got up the hill.

And at last all was arranged. Mr. Peterkin was seated in his chair. The other was offered to the lady from Philadelphia, but she preferred the carriage cushions; so did old Mr. Bromwick. And the table-cloth was spread,— for they did bring a table-cloth,— and the baskets were opened, and the picnic really began. The pickles had tumbled into the butter, and the spoons had been forgotten.

and the Tremletts' basket had been left on their front door-step. But nobody seemed to mind. Everybody was hungry, and everything they ate seemed of the best. The little boys were perfectly happy, and ate of all the kinds of cake. Two of the Tremletts would stand while they were eating, because they were afraid of the ants and the spiders that seemed to be crawling round. And Elizabeth Eliza had to keep poking with a fern-leaf to drive the insects out of the plates. The lady from Philadelphia was made comfortable with the cushions and shawls, leaning against a rock. Mrs. Peterkin wondered if she forgot she had been forgotten.

John Osborne said it was time for conundrums, and asked, "Why is a pastoral musical play better than the music we have here? Because one is a grasshopper, and the other is a grass-opera!"

Elizabeth Eliza said she knew a conundrum, a very funny one, one of her friends in Boston had told her. It was, "Why is —— " It began, "Why is something like —— " — no, "Why are they different?" It was something about an old woman, or else it was something about a young one. It was very funny, if she could only think what it was about, or whether it was alike or different.

The lady from Philadelphia was proposing they should guess Elizabeth Eliza's conundrum, first the question, and then the answer, when one of the Tremletts came running down the hill, and declared she had just discovered a very threatening cloud, and she was sure it was going to rain down directly. Everybody started up, though no cloud was to be seen.

There was a great looking for umbrellas and water-proofs. Then it appeared that Elizabeth Eliza had left hers, after all, though she had gone back for it twice. Mr. Peterkin knew he had not forgotten his umbrella, because he had put the whole umbrella-stand into the wagon, and it had been brought up the hill, but it proved to hold only the family canes!

There was a great cry for the "emergency basket," that had not been opened yet. Mrs. Peterkin explained how for days the family had been putting into it what might be needed, as soon as anything was thought of. Everybody stopped to see its contents. It was carefully

covered with newspapers. First came out a backgammon-board. "That would be useful," said Ann Maria, "if we have to spend the afternoon in anybody's barn."

Next, a pair of andirons. "What were they for?" "In case of needing a fire in the woods," explained Solomon John. Then came a volume of the Encyclopædia. But it was the first volume, Agamemnon now regretted, and contained only A and a part of B, and nothing about rain or showers. Next, a bag of pea-nuts, put in by the little boys, and Elizabeth Eliza's book of poetry, and a change of boots for Mr. Peterkin; a small foot-rug in case the ground should be damp; some paint-boxes of the little boys'; a box of fish-hooks for Solomon John; an ink-bottle, carefully done up in a great deal of newspaper, which was fortunate, as the ink was oozing out; some old magazines, and a blacking-bottle; and at the bottom a sun-dial. It was all very entertaining, and there seemed to be something for every occasion but  the present. Old Mr. Bromwick did not wonder the basket was so heavy. It was all so interesting that nobody but the Tremletts went down to the carriages.

The sun was shining brighter than ever, and Ann Maria insisted on setting up the sun-dial. Certainly there was no danger of a shower, and they might as well go on with the picnic. But when Solomon John and Ann Maria had arranged the sun-dial they asked everybody to look at their watches, so that they might see if it was right. And then came a great exclamation at the hour: "It was time they were all going home!"

The lady from Philadelphia had been wrapping her shawl about her, as she felt the sun was low. But nobody had any idea it was so late! Well, they had left late, and went back a great many times, had stopped sometimes to consult, and had been long on the road, and it had taken a long time to fetch up the things; so it was no wonder it was time to go away. But it had been a delightful picnic, after all.

THE PETERKINS' CHARADES.

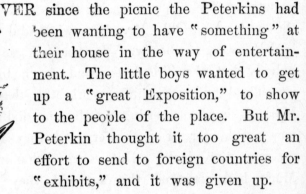

EVER since the picnic the Peterkins had been wanting to have "something" at their house in the way of entertainment. The little boys wanted to get up a "great Exposition," to show to the people of the place. But Mr. Peterkin thought it too great an effort to send to foreign countries for "exhibits," and it was given up.

There was, however, a new water-trough needed on the town common, and the ladies of the place thought it ought to be something handsome, — something more than a common trough, — and they ought to work for it.

Elizabeth Eliza had heard at Philadelphia how much women had done, and she felt they ought to contribute to such a cause. She had an idea, but she would not speak of it at first, not until after she had written to the lady from Philadelphia. She had often thought, in many cases, if they had asked her advice first, they might have saved trouble.

Still, how could they ask advice before they themselves knew what they wanted? It was very easy to
ask advice, but you must first know what to ask about.
And again: Elizabeth Eliza felt you might have ideas,
but you could not always put them together. There was
this idea of the water-trough,
and then this idea of getting
some money for it. So she began with writing to the lady
from Philadelphia. The little
boys believed she spent enough
for it in postage-stamps before
it all came out.

But it did come out at
last that the Peterkins were to
have some charades at their
own house for the benefit of the needed water-trough, —
tickets sold only to especial friends. Ann Maria Bromwick was to help act, because she could bring some old
bonnets and gowns that had been worn by an aged aunt
years ago, and which they had always kept. Elizabeth
Eliza said that Solomon John would have to be a Turk,
and they must borrow all the red things and cashmere
scarfs in the place. She knew people would be willing
to lend things.

Agamemnon thought you ought to get in something
about the Hindoos, they were such an odd people. Elizabeth Eliza said you must not have it too odd, or people

would not understand it, and she did not want anything to frighten her mother. She had one word suggested by the lady from Philadelphia in her letters, — the one that had "Turk" in it, — but they ought to have two words.

"Oh, yes," Ann Maria said, "you must have two words; if the people paid for their tickets they would want to get their money's worth."

Solomon John thought you might have "Hindoos"; the little boys could color their faces brown, to look like Hindoos. You could have the first scene an Irishman catching a hen, and then paying the water-taxes for "dues," and then have the little boys for Hindoos.

A great many other words were talked of, but nothing seemed to suit. There was a curtain, too, to be thought of, because the folding-doors stuck when you tried to open and shut them. Agamemnon said that the Pan-Elocutionists had a curtain they would probably lend John Osborne, and so it was decided to ask John Osborne to help.

If they had a curtain they ought to have a stage. Solomon John said he was sure he had boards and nails enough, and it would be easy to make a stage if John Osborne would help put it up.

All this talk was the day before the charades. In

the midst of it Ann Maria went over for her old bonnets and dresses and umbrellas, and they spent the evening in trying on the various things, — such odd caps and remarkable bonnets! Solomon John said they ought to have plenty of bandboxes; if you only had bandboxes enough a charade was sure to go off well; he had seen charades in Boston. Mrs. Peterkin said there were plenty in their attic, and the little boys brought down piles of them, and the back parlor was filled with costumes.

Ann Maria said she could bring over more things if she only knew what they were going to act. Elizabeth Eliza told her to bring anything she had, — it would all come of use.

The morning came, and the boards were collected for the stage. Agamemnon and Solomon John gave themselves to the work, and John Osborne helped zealously. He said the Pan-Elocutionists would lend a scene also. There was a great clatter of bandboxes, and piles of shawls in corners, and such a piece of work in getting up the curtain! In the midst of it came in the little boys, shouting, "All the tickets are sold, at ten cents each!"

"Seventy tickets sold!" exclaimed Agamemnon.

"Seven dollars for the water-trough!" said Elizabeth Eliza.

"And we do not know yet what we are going to act!" exclaimed Ann Maria.

But everybody's attention had to be given to the

scene that was going up in the background, borrowed from the Pan-Elocutionists. It was magnificent, and represented a forest.

"Where are we going to put seventy people?" exclaimed Mrs. Peterkin, venturing, dismayed, into the heaps of shavings, and boards, and litter.

The little boys exclaimed that a large part of the audience consisted of boys, who would not take up much room. But how much clearing and sweeping and moving of chairs was necessary before all could be made ready! It was late, and some of the people had already come to secure good seats, even before the actors had assembled.

"What are we going to act?" asked Ann Maria.

"I have been so torn with one thing and another," said Elizabeth Eliza, "I haven't had time to think!"

"Haven't you the word yet?" asked John Osborne, for the audience was flocking in, and the seats were filling up rapidly.

"I have got one word in my pocket," said Elizabeth Eliza, "in the letter from the lady from Philadelphia. She sent me the parts of the word. Solomon John is to be a Turk, but I don't yet understand the whole of the word."

"You don't know the word, and the people are all here!" said John Osborne, impatiently.

"Elizabeth Eliza!" exclaimed Ann Maria, "Solomon John says I'm to be a Turkish slave, and I'll have to wear a veil. Do you know where the veils are? You know I brought them over last night."

"Elizabeth Eliza! Solomon John wants you to send him the large cashmere scarf!" exclaimed one of the little boys, coming in. "Elizabeth Eliza! you must tell us what kind of faces to make up!" cried another of the boys.

And the audience were heard meanwhile taking their seats on the other side of the thin curtain.

"You sit in front, Mrs. Bromwick; you are a little hard of hearing; sit where you can hear."

"And let Julia Fitch come where she can see," said another voice.

"And we have not any words for them to hear or see!" exclaimed John Osborne, behind the curtain.

"Oh, I wish we'd never determined to have charades!" exclaimed Elizabeth Eliza. "Can't we return the money?"

"They are all here; we must give them something!" said John Osborne, heroically.

"And Solomon John is almost dressed," reported Ann Maria, winding a veil around her head.

"Why don't we take Solomon John's word 'Hindoos' for the first?" said Agamemnon.

John Osborne agreed to go in the first, hunting the "hin," or anything, and one of the little boys took the part of the hen, with the help of a feather duster. The bell rang, and the first scene began.

It was a great success. John Osborne's Irish was

perfect. Nobody guessed the word, for the hen crowed
by mistake; but it received great applause.

Mr. Peterkin came on in the second scene to receive
the water-rates, and made a long speech on taxation. He
was interrupted by Ann Maria as an old woman in a huge
bonnet. She persisted in turning her back to the audience,
speaking so low nobody heard her; and Elizabeth Eliza,
who appeared in a more remarkable bonnet, was so alarmed
she went directly back, saying she had forgotten something.
But this was supposed to be the effect intended, and it
was loudly cheered.

Then came a long delay, for the little boys brought
out a number of their friends to be browned for Hindoos.
Ann Maria played on the piano till the scene was ready.
The curtain rose upon five brown boys done up in blankets
and turbans.

"I am thankful that is over," said Elizabeth Eliza,
"for now we can act my word. Only I don't myself
know the whole."

"Never mind, let us act it," said John Osborne, "and
the audience can guess the whole."

"The first syllable must be the letter P," said Elizabeth Eliza, "and we must have a school."

Agamemnon was master, and the little boys and their
friends went on as scholars. All the boys talked and
shouted at once, acting their idea of a school by flinging
pea-nuts about, and scoffing at the master.

"They'll guess that to be 'row,'" said John Osborne, in despair; "they'll never guess 'P'!"

The next scene was gorgeous. Solomon John, as a Turk, reclined on John Osborne's army-blanket. He had on a turban, and a long beard, and all the family shawls. Ann Maria and Elizabeth Eliza were brought in to him, veiled, by the little boys in their Hindoo costumes.

This was considered the great scene of the evening, though Elizabeth Eliza was sure she did not know what to do, — whether to kneel or sit down; she did not know whether Turkish women did sit down, and she could not help laughing whenever she looked at Solomon John. He, however, kept his solemnity. "I suppose I need not say much," he had said, "for I shall be the 'Turk who was dreaming of the hour.'" But he did order the little boys to bring sherbet, and when they brought it without ice insisted they must have their heads cut off, and Ann Maria fainted, and the scene closed.

"What are we to do now?" asked John Osborne, warming up to the occasion.

"We must have an 'inn' scene," said Elizabeth Eliza, consulting her letter; "two inns, if we can."

"We will have some travellers disgusted with one inn, and going to another," said John Osborne.

"Now is the time for the bandboxes," said Solomon John, who, since his Turk scene was over, could give his attention to the rest of the charade.

Elizabeth Eliza and Ann Maria went on as rival hostesses, trying to draw Solomon John, Agamemnon, and John Osborne into their several inns. The little boys carried valises, hand-bags, umbrellas, and bandboxes. Bandbox after bandbox appeared, and when Agamemnon sat down upon his the applause was immense. At last the curtain fell.

"Now for the whole," said John Osborne, as he made his way off the stage over a heap of umbrellas.

"I can't think why the lady from Philadelphia did not send me the whole," said Elizabeth Eliza, musing over the letter.

"Listen, they are guessing," said John Osborne. "'*D-ice-box.*' I don't wonder they get it wrong."

"But we know it can't be that!" exclaimed Elizabeth Eliza, in agony. "How can we act the whole if we don't know it ourselves?"

"Oh, I see it!" said Ann Maria, clapping her hands. "Get your whole family in for the last scene."

Mr. and Mrs. Peterkin were summoned to the stage, and formed the background, standing on stools; in front were Agamemnon and Solomon John, leaving room for Elizabeth Eliza between; a little in advance, and in front of all, half kneeling, were the little boys, in their india-rubber boots.

The audience rose to an exclamation of delight, "The Peterkins!" "P-Turk-Inns!"

It was not until this moment that Elizabeth Eliza guessed the whole.

"What a tableau!" exclaimed Mr. Bromwick; "the Peterkin family guessing their own charade."

THE PETERKINS ARE OBLIGED TO MOVE.

GAMEMNON had long felt it an impropriety to live in a house that was called a " semi-detached " house, when there was no other " semi " to it. It had always remained wholly detached, as the owner had never built the other half. Mrs. Peterkin felt this was not a sufficient reason for undertaking the terrible process of a move to another house, when they were fully satisfied with the one they were in.

But a more powerful reason forced them to go. The track of a new railroad had to be carried directly through the place, and a station was to be built on that very spot.

Mrs. Peterkin so much dreaded moving that she questioned whether they could not continue to live in the upper part of the house and give up the lower part to the station. They could then dine at the restaurant, and it would be very convenient about travelling, as there would be no danger of missing the train, if one were sure of the direction.

But when the track was actually laid by the side of the house, and the steam-engine of the construction train puffed and screamed under the dining-room windows, and the engineer calmly looked in to see what the family had for dinner, she felt, indeed, that they must move.

But where should they go? It was difficult to find a house that satisfied the whole family. One was too far off, and looked into a tan-pit; another was too much in the m'ddle of the town, next door to a machine-shop. Elizabeth Eliza wanted a porch covered with vines, that should face the sunset; while Mr. Peterkin thought it would not be convenient to sit there looking towards the west in the late afternoon (which was his only leisure time), for the sun would shine in his face. The little boys wanted a house with a great many doors, so that they could go in and out often. But Mr. Peterkin did not like so much slamming, and felt there was more danger of burglars with so many doors. Agamemnon wanted an observatory, and Solomon John a shed for a workshop. If he could have carpenters' tools and a workbench he could build an observatory, if it were wanted.

But it was necessary to decide upon something, for they must leave their house directly. So they were obliged to take Mr. Finch's, at the Corners. It satisfied none of the family. The porch was a piazza, and was opposite a barn. There were three other doors. — too many to please Mr. Peterkin, and not enough for the little boys. There

was no observatory, and nothing to observe if there were
one, as the house was too low,

and some high trees shut out any
view. Elizabeth Eliza had hoped
for a view; but Mr. Peterkin consoled her by deciding it was more
healthy to have to walk for a view,
and Mrs. Peterkin agreed that they might get tired of
the same every day.

And everybody was glad a selection
was made, and the little boys carried
their india-rubber boots the very first
afternoon.

Elizabeth Eliza wanted to have some
system in the moving, and spent the
evening in drawing up a plan. It would
be easy to arrange everything beforehand,
so that there should not be the con-

fusion that her mother dreaded, and the discomfort they
had in their last move. Mrs. Peterkin shook her head;

she did not think it possible to move with
any comfort. Agamemnon said a great deal
could be done with a list and a programme.

Elizabeth Eliza declared if all were
well arranged a programme would make it
perfectly easy. They were to have new
parlor carpets, which could be put down
in the new house the first thing. Then the parlor

furniture could be moved in, and there would be two comfortable rooms, in which Mr. and Mrs. Peterkin could sit while the rest of the move went on. Then the old parlor carpets could be taken up for the new dining-room and the downstairs bedroom, and the family could meanwhile dine at the old house. Mr. Peterkin did not object to this, though the distance was considerable, as he felt exercise would be good for them all. Elizabeth Eliza's programme then arranged that the dining-room furniture should be moved the third day, by which time one of the old parlor carpets would be down in the new dining-room, and they could still sleep in the old house. Thus there would always be a quiet, comfortable place in one house or the other. Each night, when Mr. Peterkin came home, he would find some place for quiet thought and rest, and each day there should be moved only the furniture needed for a certain room. Great confusion would be avoided and nothing misplaced. Elizabeth Eliza wrote these last words at the head of her programme, — "Misplace nothing." And Agamemnon made a copy of the programme for each member of the family.

The first thing to be done was to buy the parlor carpets. Elizabeth Eliza had already looked at some in Boston, and the next morning she went, by an early train, with her father, Agamemnon, and Solomon John, to decide upon them.

They got home about eleven o'clock, and when they reached the house were dismayed to find two furniture wagons in front of the gate, already partly filled! Mrs.

Peterkin was walking in and out of the open door, a large book in one hand, and a duster in the other, and she came to meet them in an agony of anxiety. What should they do? The furniture carts had appeared soon after the rest had left for Boston, and the men had insisted upon beginning to move the things. In vain had she shown Elizabeth Eliza's programme; in vain had she insisted they must take only the parlor furniture. They had declared they must put the heavy pieces in the bottom of the cart, and the lighter furniture on top. So she had seen them go into every room in the house, and select one piece of furniture after another, without even looking at Elizabeth Eliza's programme; she doubted if they could have read it if they had looked at it.

Mr. Peterkin had ordered the carters to come; but he had no idea they would come so early, and supposed it would take them a long time to fill the carts.

But they had taken the dining-room sideboard first, — a heavy piece of furniture, — and all its contents were now on the dining-room tables. Then, indeed, they selected the parlor book-case, but had set every book on the floor. The men had told Mrs. Peterkin they would put the books in the bottom of the cart, very much in the order they were taken from the shelves. But by this time Mrs. Peterkin was considering the carters as natural enemies, and dared not trust them; besides, the books ought all to be dusted. So she was now holding one of the volumes of Agamemnon's Encyclopædia, with difficulty, in one hand, while she was dusting it with the other. Elizabeth Eliza was in dismay. At this moment four men were bringing down a large chest of drawers from her father's room, and they called to her to stand out of the way. The parlors were a scene of confusion. In dusting the books Mrs. Peterkin neglected to restore them to the careful rows in which they were left by the men, and they lay in hopeless masses in different parts of the room. Elizabeth Eliza sunk in despair upon the end of a sofa.

"It would have been better to buy the red and blue carpet," said Solomon John.

"Is not the carpet bought?" exclaimed Mrs. Peterkin. And then they were obliged to confess they had been unable to decide upon one, and had come back to consult Mrs. Peterkin.

"What shall we do?" asked Mrs. Peterkin.

Elizabeth Eliza rose from the sofa and went to the door, saying, "I shall be back in a moment."

Agamemnon slowly passed round the room, collecting the scattered volumes of his Encyclopædia. Mr. Peterkin offered a helping hand to a man lifting a wardrobe.

Elizabeth Eliza soon returned. "I did not like to go

and ask her. But I felt that I must in such an emer‑
gency. I explained to her the whole matter, and she
thinks we should take the carpet at Makillan's."

"Makillan's" was a store in the village, and the carpet
was the only one all the family had liked without any
doubt; but they had supposed they might prefer one from
Boston.

The moment was a critical one. Solomon John was
sent directly to Makillan's to order the carpet to be put
down that very day. But where should they dine? where
should they have their supper? and where was Mr. Peter‑
kin's "quiet hour"? Elizabeth Eliza was frantic; the
dining‑room floor and table were covered with things.

It was decided that Mr. and Mrs. Peterkin should
dine at the Bromwicks, who had been most neighborly
in their offers, and the rest should get something to eat
at the baker's.

Agamemnon and Elizabeth Eliza hastened away to be
ready to receive the carts at the other house, and direct
the furniture as they could. After all there was some‑
thing exhilarating in this opening of the new house, and
in deciding where things should go. Gayly Elizabeth
Eliza stepped down the front garden of the new home
and across the piazza, and to the door. But it was locked,
and she had no keys!

"Agamemnon, did you bring the keys?" she exclaimed.

No, he had not seen them since the morning, — when
— ah! — yes, the little boys were allowed to go to the house

for their india-rubber boots, as there was a threatening of rain. Perhaps they had left some door unfastened — perhaps they had put the keys under the door-mat. No, each door, each window, was solidly closed, and there was no mat!

"I shall have to go to the school to see if they took the keys with them," said Agamemnon; "or else go home to see if they left them there." The school was in a different direction from the house, and far at the other end of the town; for Mr. Peterkin had not yet changed the boys' school, as he proposed to do after their move.

"That will be the only way," said Elizabeth Eliza; for it had been arranged that the little boys should take their lunch to school, and not come home at noon.

She sat down on the steps to wait, but only for a moment, for the carts soon appeared, turning the corner. What should be done with the furniture? Of course the carters must wait for the keys, as she should need them to set the furniture up in the right places. But they could not stop for this. They put it down upon the piazza, on the steps, in the garden, and Elizabeth Eliza saw how incongruous it was! There was something from every room in the house! Even the large family chest, which had proved too heavy for them to travel with, had come down from the attic, and stood against the front door.

And Solomon John appeared with the carpet woman,

and a boy with a wheelbarrow, bringing the new carpet.

And all stood and waited. Some opposite neighbors appeared to offer advice and look on, and Elizabeth Eliza groaned inwardly that only the shabbiest of their furniture appeared to be standing full in view.

It seemed ages before Agamemnon returned, and no wonder; for he had been to the house, then to the school, then back to the house, for one of the little boys had left the keys at home, in the pocket of his clothes. Meanwhile the carpet-woman had waited, and the boy with the wheelbarrow had waited, and when they got in they found the parlor must be swept and cleaned. So the carpet-woman went off in dudgeon, for she was sure there would not be time enough to do anything.

And one of the carts came again, and in their hurry the men set the furniture down anywhere. Elizabeth Eliza was hoping to make a little place in the dining-room, where they might have their supper, and go home to sleep. But she looked out, and there were the carters bringing the bedsteads, and proceeding to carry them upstairs.

In despair Elizabeth Eliza went back to the old house. If she had been there she might have prevented this. She found Mrs. Peterkin in an agony about the entry oil-cloth. It had been made in the house, and how could it be taken out of the house? Agamemnon made measurements; it certainly could not go out of the front door! He suggested it might be left till the house was pulled down, when it could easily be moved out of one side. But Elizabeth Eliza reminded him that the whole house was to be moved without being taken apart. Perhaps it could be cut in strips narrow enough to go out. One of the men loading the remaining cart disposed of the question by coming in and rolling up the oil-cloth and carrying it off on top of his wagon.

Elizabeth Eliza felt she must hurry back to the new house. But what should they do? — no beds here, no carpets there! The dining-room table and sideboard were at the other house, the plates, and forks, and spoons here. In vain she looked at her programme. It was all reversed; everything was misplaced. Mr. Peterkin would suppose they were to eat here and sleep here, and what had become of the little boys?

Meanwhile the man with the first cart had returned. They fell to packing the dining-room china.

They were up in the attic, they were down in the cellar. Even one suggested to take the tacks out of the parlor carpets, as they should want to take them next. Mrs. Peterkin sunk upon a kitchen chair.

"Oh, I wish we had decided to stay and be moved in the house!" she exclaimed.

Solomon John urged his mother to go to the new house, for Mr. Peterkin would be there for his "quiet hour." And when the carters at last appeared, carrying the parlor carpets on their shoulders, she sighed and said,

"There is nothing left," and meekly consented to be led away.

They reached the new house to find Mr. Peterkin sitting calmly in a rocking-chair on the piazza, watching the oxen coming into the opposite barn. He was waiting for the keys, which Solomon John had taken back with him. The little boys were in a horse-chestnut tree, at the side of the house.

Agamemnon opened the door. The passages were crowded with furniture, the floors were strewn with books; the bureau was upstairs that was to stand in a lower bedroom; there was not a place to lay a table, — there was nothing to lay upon it; for the knives and plates and spoons had not come, and although the tables were there they were covered with chairs and boxes.

At this moment came a covered basket from the lady from Philadelphia. It contained a choice supper, and forks and spoons, and at the same moment appeared a pot of hot tea from an opposite neighbor. They placed all this on the back of a bookcase lying upset, and sat around it. Solomon John came rushing in from the gate.

"The last load is coming! We are all moved!" he exclaimed; and the little boys joined in a chorus, "We are moved! we are moved!"

Mrs. Peterkin looked sadly round; the kitchen utensils were lying on the parlor lounge, and an old family gun on Elizabeth Eliza's hat-box. The parlor clock stood on a barrel; some coal-scuttles had been placed on the parlor table, a bust of Washington stood in the door-way, and the looking-glasses leaned against the pillars of the piazza. But they were moved! Mrs. Peterkin felt, indeed, that they were very much moved.

THE PETERKINS DECIDE TO LEARN THE LANGUAGES.

ERTAINLY now was the time to study the languages. The Peterkins had moved into a new house, far more convenient than their old one, where they would have a place for everything and everything in its place. Of course they would then have more time.

Elizabeth Eliza recalled the troubles of the old house; how for a long time she was obliged to sit outside of the window upon the piazza, when she wanted to play on her piano.

Mrs. Peterkin reminded them of the difficulty about the table-cloths. The upper table-cloth was kept in a trunk that had to stand in front of the door to the closet under the stairs. But the under table-cloth was kept in a drawer in the closet. So, whenever the cloths were changed, the trunk had to be pushed away under some projecting shelves to make room for opening the closet-door (as the under table-cloth must be taken out first), then the trunk was pushed back to make room for it to be opened for the upper table-cloth, and, after all, it was necessary to push the trunk away again to open the closet-door for the knife-tray. This always consumed a great deal of time.

Now that the china-closet was large enough, everything could find a place in it.

Agamemnon especially enjoyed the new library. In the old house there was no separate room for books. The dictionaries were kept upstairs, which was very inconvenient, and the volumes of the Encyclopædia could not be together. There was not room for all in one place. So from A to P were to be found downstairs, and from Q to Z were scattered in different rooms upstairs. And the worst of it was, you could never remember whether from A to P included P. "I always went upstairs after P," said Agamemnon, "and then always found it downstairs, or else it was the other way."

Of course, now there were more conveniences for study. With the books all in one room there would be no time wasted in looking for them.

Mr. Peterkin suggested they should each take a separate language. If they went abroad this would prove a great convenience. Elizabeth Eliza could talk French with the Parisians; Agamemnon, German with the Germans; Solomon John, Italian with the Italians; Mrs. Peterkin, Spanish in Spain; and perhaps he could himself master all the Eastern languages and Russian.

Mrs. Peterkin was uncertain about undertaking the Spanish; but all the family felt very sure they should not go to Spain (as Elizabeth Eliza dreaded the Inquisition), and Mrs. Peterkin felt more willing.

Still she had quite an objection to going abroad. She had always said she would not go till a bridge was made across the Atlantic, and she was sure it did not look like it now.

Agamemnon said there was no knowing. There was something new every day, and a bridge was surely not harder to invent than a telephone, for they had bridges in the very earliest days.

Then came up the question of the teachers. Probably these could be found in Boston. If they could all come the same day three could be brought out in the carryall. Agamemnon could go in for them, and could learn a little on the way out and in.

Mr. Peterkin made some inquiries about the Oriental languages. He was told that Sanscrit was at the root of all. So he proposed they should all begin with Sanscrit. They would thus require but one teacher, and could branch out into the other languages afterward.

But the family preferred learning the separate languages. Elizabeth Eliza already knew something of the French. She had tried to talk it, without much success, at the Centennial Exhibition, at one of the side-stands. But she found she had been talking with a Moorish gentleman who did not understand French. Mr. Peterkin feared they might need more libraries if all the teachers came at the same hour; but Agamemnon reminded him that they would be using different dictionaries. And Mr. Peterkin thought something might be learned by having them all at once. Each one might pick up something beside the language he was studying, and it was a great thing to learn to talk a foreign language while others were talking about you. Mrs. Peterkin was afraid it would be like the Tower of Babel, and hoped it was all right.

Agamemnon brought forward another difficulty. Of course they ought to have foreign teachers, who spoke only their native languages. But, in this case, how could they engage them to come, or explain to them about the carryall, or arrange the proposed hours? He did not understand how anybody ever began with a foreigner, because he could not even tell him what he wanted.

Elizabeth Eliza thought a great deal might be done by signs and pantomime. Solomon John and the little boys began to show how it might be done. Elizabeth Eliza explained how "*langues*" meant both "languages" and "tongues," and they could point to their tongues. For practice, the little boys represented the foreign teachers talking in their different languages, and Agamemnon and Solomon John went to invite them to come out and teach the family by a series of signs.

Mr. Peterkin thought their success was admirable, and

that they might almost go abroad without any study of the languages, and trust to explaining themselves by signs. Still, as the bridge was not yet made, it might be as well to wait and cultivate the languages.

Mrs. Peterkin was afraid the foreign teachers might imagine they were invited out to lunch. Solomon John had constantly pointed to his mouth as he opened it and shut it, putting out his tongue; and it looked a great deal more as if he were inviting them to eat than asking them to teach. Agamemnon suggested that they might carry the separate dictionaries when they went to see the teachers, and that would show that they meant lessons, and not lunch.

Mrs. Peterkin was not sure but she ought to prepare a lunch for them, if they had come all that way; but she certainly did not know what they were accustomed to eat.

Mr. Peterkin thought this would be a good thing to learn of the foreigners. It would be a good preparation for going abroad, and they might get used to the dishes before starting. The little boys were delighted at the idea of having new things cooked. Agamemnon had heard that beer-soup was a favorite dish with the Germans, and he would inquire how it was made in the first lesson. Solomon John had heard they were all very fond of garlic, and thought it would be a pretty attention to have some in the house the first day, that they might be cheered by the odor.

Elizabeth Eliza wanted to surprise the lady from Philadelphia by her knowledge of French, and hoped to begin on her lessons before the Philadelphia family arrived for their annual visit.

There were still some delays. Mr. Peterkin was very anxious to obtain teachers who had been but a short time in this country. He did not want to be tempted to talk any English with them. He wanted the latest and freshest languages, and at last came home one day with a list of "brand-new foreigners."

They decided to borrow the Bromwicks' carryall to use, beside their own, for the first day, and Mr. Peterkin and Agamemnon drove into town to bring all the teachers out. One was a Russian gentleman, travelling, who came with no idea of giving lessons, but perhaps he would consent to do so. He could not yet speak English.

Mr. Peterkin had his card-case, and the cards of the several gentlemen who had recommended the different teachers, and he went with Agamemnon from hotel to hotel collecting them. He found them all very polite, and ready to come, after the explanation by signs agreed upon. The dictionaries had been forgotten, but Agamemnon had a directory, which looked the same, and seemed to satisfy the foreigners.

Mr. Peterkin was obliged to content himself with the Russian instead of one who could teach Sanscrit, as there was no new teacher of that language lately arrived.

But there was an unexpected difficulty in getting the Russian gentleman into the same carriage with the teacher of Arabic, for he was a Turk, sitting with a fez on his head, on the back seat! They glared at each other, and began to assail each other in every language they knew, none of which Mr. Peterkin could understand. It might be Russian; it might be Arabic. It was easy to understand that they would never consent to sit in the same carriage. Mr. Peterkin was in despair; he had forgotten about the Russian war! What a mistake to have invited the Turk!

Quite a crowd collected on the sidewalk in front of the hotel. But the French gentleman politely, but stiffly, invited the Russian to go with him in the first carryall. Here was another difficulty. For the German professor was quietly ensconced on the back seat! As soon as the French gentleman put his foot on the step and saw him he addressed him in such forcible language that the German professor got out of the door the other  side, and came round on the sidewalk and took him by the collar. Certainly the German and French gen-

tlemen could not be put together, and more crowd collected!

Agamemnon, however, had happily studied up the
German word "Herr," and he ap-
plied it to the German, inviting
him by signs to take a seat in
the other carryall. The German
consented to sit by the Turk, as
they neither of them could understand the other; and at last they
started, Mr. Peterkin with the
Italian by his side, and the French
and Russian teachers behind, vociferating to each other in
languages unknown to Mr. Peterkin, while he feared they
were not perfectly in harmony; so he drove home as fast
as possible. Agamemnon had a silent party. The Spaniard by his side was a little moody, while the Turk and
the German behind did not utter a word.

At last they reached the house,
and were greeted by Mrs. Peterkin
and Elizabeth Eliza, Mrs. Peterkin
with her llama lace shawl over her
shoulders, as a tribute to the Spanish
teacher. Mr. Peterkin was careful to
take his party in first, and deposit
them in a distant part of the library,
far from the Turk or the German,
even putting the Frenchman and Russian apart.

Solomon John found the Italian dictionary, and seated himself by his Italian; Agamemnon, with the German dictionary, by the German. The little boys took their copy of the "Arabian Nights" to the Turk. Mr. Peterkin attempted to explain to the Russian that he had no Russian dictionary, as he had hoped to learn Sanscrit of him, while Mrs. Peterkin was trying to inform her

teacher that she had no books in Spanish. She got over all fears of the Inquisition, he looked so sad, and she tried to talk a little, using English words, but very slowly, and altering the accent as far as she knew how. The Spaniard bowed, looked gravely interested, and was very polite.

Elizabeth Eliza, meanwhile, was trying her grammar phrases with the Parisian. She found it easier to talk French than to understand him. But he understood perfectly her sentences. She repeated one of her vocabularies, and went on with, "*J'ai le livre.*" "*As-tu le pain?*" "*L'enfant a une poire.*" He listened with great attention, and replied slowly. Suddenly she started after making out one of his sentences, and went to her mother to whisper, "They have made the mistake you feared. They think they are invited to lunch! *He* has just been thanking me for our politeness in inviting them to *déjeûner,* — that means breakfast!"

"They have not had their breakfast!" exclaimed Mrs.
Peterkin, looking at her Spaniard;
"he does look hungry! What shall
we do?"

Elizabeth Eliza was consulting
her father. What should they do?
How should they make them understand that they invited them to
teach, not lunch. Elizabeth Eliza
begged Agamemnon to look out
"*apprendre*" in the dictionary. It
must mean to teach. Alas, they found it means both to
teach and to learn! What should they do? The foreigners were now sitting silent in their different corners.
The Spaniard grew more and more sallow. What if he
should faint? The Frenchman was rolling up each of his
mustaches to a point as he gazed at the German. What
if the Russian should fight the Turk? What if the
German should be exasperated by the airs of the Parisian?

"We must give them something to eat," said Mr.
Peterkin, in a low tone. "It would calm them."

"If I only knew what they were used to eating,"
said Mrs. Peterkin.

Solomon John suggested that none of them knew
what the others were used to eating, and they might
bring in anything.

Mrs. Peterkin hastened out with hospitable intents. Amanda could make good coffee. Mr. Peterkin had suggested some American dish. Solomon John sent a little boy for some olives.

It was not long before the coffee came in, and a dish of baked beans. Next, some olives and a loaf of bread, and some boiled eggs, and some bottles of beer. The effect was astonishing. Every man spoke his own tongue, and fluently. Mrs. Peterkin poured out coffee for the Spaniard, while he bowed to her. They all liked beer; they all liked olives. The Frenchman was fluent about " *les mœurs Américaines.*" Elizabeth Eliza supposed he alluded to their not having set any table. The Turk smiled; the Russian was voluble. In the midst of the clang of the different languages, just as Mr. Peterkin was again repeating, under cover of the noise of many tongues, "How shall we make them understand that we want them to teach?" — at this very moment the door was flung open, and there came in the lady from Philadelphia, that day arrived, her first call of the season.

She started back in terror at the tumult of so many different languages. The family, with joy, rushed to meet her. All together they called upon her to explain for them. Could she help them? Could she tell the foreigners they wanted to take lessons? Lessons? They had no sooner uttered the word than their guests all started up with faces beaming with joy. It was the one English

word they all knew! They had come to Boston to give
lessons! The Russian traveller had hoped to learn English
in this way. The thought pleased them more than the
déjeûner. Yes, gladly would they give lessons. The Turk
smiled at the idea. The first step was taken. The teachers knew they were expected to teach.

MODERN IMPROVEMENTS AT THE PETERKINS'.

GAMEMNON felt that it became necessary for him to choose a profession. It was important on account of the little boys. If he should make a trial of several different professions he could find out which would be the most likely to be successful, and it would then be easy to bring up the little boys in the right direction.

Elizabeth Eliza agreed with this. She thought the family occasionally made mistakes, and had come near disgracing themselves. Now was their chance to avoid this in future by giving the little boys a proper education.

Solomon John was almost determined to become a doctor. From earliest childhood he had practised writing recipes on little slips of paper. Mrs. Peterkin, to be sure, was afraid of infection. She could not bear the idea of his bringing one disease after the other into the family circle. Solomon John, too, did not like sick people. He thought he might manage it if he should not have to see his patients while they were sick. If he could only visit them when they were recovering, and when the danger of infection was over, he would really enjoy making calls.

He should have a comfortable doctor's chaise, and take one of the little boys to hold his horse while he went in, and he thought he could get through the conversational part very well, and feeling the pulse, perhaps looking at the tongue. He should  take and read all the newspapers, and so be thoroughly acquainted with the news of the day to talk of. But he should not like to be waked up at night to visit. Mr. Peterkin thought that would not be necessary. He had seen signs on doors of "Night Doctor," and certainly it would be as convenient to have a sign of "Not a Night Doctor."

Solomon John thought he might write his advice to those of his patients who were dangerously ill, from whom there was danger of infection. And then Elizabeth Eliza agreed that his prescriptions would probably be so satisfactory that they would keep his patients well, — not too well to do without a doctor, but needing his recipes.

Agamemnon was delayed, however, in his choice of a profession, by a desire he had to become a famous inventor. If he could only invent something important, and get out a patent, he would make himself known all over the country. If he could get out a patent he would be set up for life, or at least as long as the patent lasted, and it would be well to be sure to arrange it to last through his natural life.

Indeed, he had gone so far as to make his invention. It had been suggested by their trouble with a key, in their late moving to their new house. He had studied the matter over a great deal. He looked it up in the Encyclopædia, and had spent a day or two in the Public Library, in reading about Chubb's Lock and other patent locks.

But his plan was more simple. It was this: that all keys should be made alike! He wondered it had not been thought of before; but so it was, Solomon John said, with all inventions, with Christopher Columbus, and everybody. Nobody knew the invention till it was invented, and then it looked very simple. With Agamemnon's plan you need have but one key, that should fit everything! It should be a medium-sized key, not too large to carry. It ought to answer for a house door, but you might open a portmanteau with it. How much less danger there would be of losing one's keys if there were only one to lose!

Mrs. Peterkin thought it would be inconvenient if their father were out, and she wanted to open the jam-closet for the little boys. But Agamemnon explained that he did not mean there should be but one key in the family, or in a town, — you might have as many as you pleased, only they should all be alike.

Elizabeth Eliza felt it would be a great convenience, — they could keep the front door always locked, yet she could open it with the key of her upper drawer; that she was sure to have with her.  And Mrs. Peterkin felt it might be a convenience if they had one on each story, so that they need not go up and down for it.

Mr. Peterkin studied all the papers and advertisements, to decide about the lawyer whom they should consult, and at last, one morning, they went into town to visit a patent-agent.

Elizabeth Eliza took the occasion to make a call upon the lady from Philadelphia, but she came back hurriedly to her mother.

"I have had a delightful call," she said; "but — perhaps I was wrong — I could not help, in conversation, speaking of Agamemnon's proposed patent. I ought not to have mentioned it, as such things are kept profound secrets; they say women always do tell things; I suppose that is the reason."

"But where is the harm?" asked Mrs. Peterkin. "I'm sure you can trust the lady from Philadelphia."

Elizabeth Eliza then explained that the lady from Philadelphia had questioned the plan a little when it was told her. and had suggested that "if everybody had the same key there would be no particular use in a lock."

"Did you explain to her," said Mrs. Peterkin, "that we were not all to have the same keys?"

"I couldn't quite understand her," said Elizabeth Eliza, "but she seemed to think that burglars and other people might come in if the keys were the same."

"Agamemnon would not sell his patent to burglars!" said Mrs. Peterkin, indignantly.

"But about other people," said Elizabeth Eliza; "there is my upper drawer; the little boys might open it at Christmas-time, — and their presents in it!"

"And I am not sure that I could trust Amanda," said Mrs. Peterkin, considering.

Both she and Elizabeth Eliza felt that Mr. Peterkin ought to know what the lady from Philadelphia had suggested. Elizabeth Eliza then proposed going into town, but it would take so long she might not reach them in time. A telegram would be better, and she ventured to suggest using the Telegraph Alarm.

For, on moving into their new house, they had discovered it was provided with all the modern improvements. This had been a disappointment to Mrs

Peterkin, for she was afraid of them, since their experience the last winter, when their water-pipes were frozen up. She had been originally attracted to the house by an old pump at the side, which had led her to believe there were no modern improvements. It had pleased the little boys, too. They liked to pump the handle up and down, and agreed to pump all the water needed, and bring it into the house.

There was an old well, with a picturesque well-sweep, in a corner by the barn. Mrs. Peterkin was frightened by this at first. She was afraid the little boys would be falling in every day. And they showed great fondness for pulling the bucket up and down. It proved, however, that the well was dry. There was  no water in it; so she had some moss thrown down, and an old feather-bed, for safety, and the old well was a favorite place of amusement.

The house, it had proved, was well furnished with bath-rooms, and "set-waters" everywhere. Water-pipes and gas-pipes all over the house; and a hack-, telegraph-, and fire-alarm, with a little knob for each.

Mrs. Peterkin was very anxious. She feared the little boys would be summoning somebody all the time, and it was decided to conceal from them the use of the knobs, and

the card of directions at the side was destroyed. Agamemnon had made one of his first inventions to help this.
He had arranged a number of similar knobs to be put in
rows in different parts of the house, to appear as if they
were intended for ornament, and had added some to the
original knobs. Mrs. Peterkin felt more secure, and Agamemnon thought of taking out a patent for this invention.

It was, therefore, with some doubt that Elizabeth
Eliza proposed sending a telegram to her father. Mrs.
Peterkin, however, was pleased with the idea. Solomon
John was out, and the little boys were at school, and she
herself would touch the knob, while Elizabeth Eliza should
write the telegram.

"I think it is the fourth knob from the beginning," she
said, looking at one of the rows of knobs.

Elizabeth Eliza was sure of this. Agamemnon, she
believed, had put three extra knobs at each end.

"But which is the end,
and which is the beginning,
— the top or the bottom?"
Mrs. Peterkin asked hope-
lessly.

Still she bravely se-
lected a knob, and Eliza-
beth Eliza hastened with
her to look out for the
messenger. How soon
should they see the telegraph boy?

They seemed to have scarcely reached the window, when a terrible noise was heard, and down the shady street the white horses of the fire-brigade were seen rushing at a fatal speed!

It was a terrific moment!

"I have touched the fire-alarm," Mrs. Peterkin exclaimed.

Both rushed to open the front door in agony. By this time the fire-engines were approaching.

"Do not be alarmed," said the chief engineer; "the furniture shall be carefully covered, and we will move all that is necessary."

"Move again!" exclaimed Mrs. Peterkin, in agony.

Elizabeth Eliza strove to explain that she was only sending a telegram to her father, who was in Boston.

"It is not important," said the head engineer; "the fire will all be out before it could reach him."

And he ran upstairs, for the engines were beginning to play upon the roof.

Mrs. Peterkin rushed to the knobs again hurriedly; there was more necessity for summoning Mr. Peterkin home.

"Write a telegram to your father," she said to Elizabeth Eliza, "to 'come home directly.'"

"That will take but three words," said Elizabeth Eliza, with presence of mind, "and we need ten. I was just trying to make them out."

"What has come uow?" exclaimed Mrs. Peterkin, and
they hurried again to the
window, to see a row of
carriages coming down the
street.

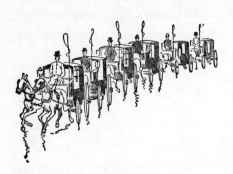

"I must have touched
the carriage-knob," cried
Mrs. Peterkin, "and I
pushed it half-a-dozen times

I felt so anxious!"

Six hacks stood before the door. All the village boys
were assembling. Even their own little boys had returned
from school, and were showing the firemen the way to
the well.

Again Mrs. Peterkin rushed to the knobs, and a fear-
ful sound arose. She had touched the burglar-alarm!

The former owner of the house, who had a great
fear of burglars, had invented a machine of his own, which
he had connected with a knob. A wire attached to the
knob moved a spring that could put in
motion a number of watchmen's rattles,
hidden under the eaves of the piazza.

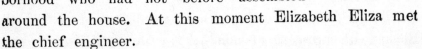

All these were now set a-going, and
their terrible din roused those of the neighborhood who had not before assembled
around the house. At this moment Elizabeth Eliza met
the chief engineer.

"You need not send for more help," he said; "we

have all the engines in town here, and have stirred up all the towns in the neighborhood; there's no use in springing any more alarms. I can't find the fire yet, but we have water pouring all over the house."

Elizabeth Eliza waved her telegram in the air.

" We are only trying to send a telegram to my father and brother, who are in town," she endeavored to explain.

" If it is necessary," said the chief engineer, " you might send it down in one of the hackney carriages. I see a number standing before the door. We'd better begin to move the heavier furniture, and some of you women might fill the carriages with smaller things."

Mrs. Peterkin was ready to fall into hysterics. She controlled herself with a supreme power, and hastened to touch another knob.

Elizabeth Eliza corrected her telegram, and decided to take the advice of the chief engineer and went to the door to give her message to one of the hackmen, when she saw a telegraph boy appear. Her mother had touched the right knob. It was the fourth from the beginning; but the beginning was at the other end!

She went out to meet the boy, when, to her joy, she saw behind him her father and Agamemnon. She clutched her telegram, and hurried toward them.

Mr. Peterkin was bewildered. Was the house on fire? If so, where were the flames?

He saw the row of carriages. Was there a funeral, or a wedding? Who was dead? Who was to be married?

He seized the telegram that Elizabeth Eliza reached to him, and read it aloud.

"Come to us directly — the house is NOT on fire!"

The chief engineer was standing on the steps.

"The house not on fire!" he exclaimed. "What are we all summoned for?"

"It is a mistake," cried Elizabeth Eliza, wringing her hands. "We touched the wrong knob; we wanted the telegraph boy!"

"We touched all the wrong knobs," exclaimed Mrs. Peterkin, from the house.

The chief engineer turned directly to give counter-directions, with a few exclamations of disgust, as the bells of distant fire-engines were heard approaching.

Solomon John appeared at this moment, and proposed taking one of the carriages, and going for a doctor for his mother, for she was now nearly ready to fall into hysterics, and Agamemnon thought to send a telegram down by the boy, for the evening papers, to announce that the Peterkins' house had not been on fire.

The crisis of the commotion had reached its height. The beds of flowers, bordered with dark-colored leaves, were trodden down by the feet of the crowd that had assembled.

The chief engineer grew more and more indignant, as he sent his men to order back the fire-engines from the neighboring towns. The collection of boys followed the procession as it went away. The fire-brigade hastily removed covers from some of the furniture, restored the rest to their places, and took away their ladders. Many neighbors remained, but Mr. Peterkin hastened into the house to attend to Mrs. Peterkin.

Elizabeth Eliza took an opportunity to question her father, before he went in, as to the success of their visit to town.

" We saw all the patent-agents," answered Mr. Peterkin, in a hollow whisper. " Not one of them will touch the patent, or have anything to do with it."

Elizabeth Eliza looked at Agamemnon, as he walked silently into the house. She would not now speak to him of the patent; but she recalled some words of Solomon John. When they were discussing the patent he had said that many an inventor had grown gray before his discovery was acknowledged by the public. Others might reap the harvest, but it came, perhaps, only when he was going to his grave.

Elizabeth Eliza looked at Agamemnon reverently, and followed him silently into the house.

AGAMEMNON'S CAREER.

HERE had apparently been some mistake in Agamemnon's education. He had been to a number of colleges, indeed, but he had never completed his course in any one. He had continually fallen into some difficulty with the authorities. It was singular, for he was of an inquiring mind, and had always tried to find out what would be expected of him, but had never hit upon the right thing.

Solomon John thought the trouble might be in what they called the elective system, where you were to choose what study you might take. This had always bewildered Agamemnon a good deal.

"And how was a feller to tell," Solomon John had asked, "whether he wanted to study a thing before he tried it? It might turn out awful hard!"

Agamemnon had always been fond of reading, from his childhood up. He was at his book all day long. Mrs. Peterkin had imagined he would come out a great scholar, because she could never get him away from his books.

And so it was in his colleges; he was always to be found in the library, reading and reading. But they were always the wrong books.

For instance: the class were required to prepare themselves on the Spartan war. This turned Agamemnon's attention to the Fenians, and to study the subject he read up on "Charles O'Malley," and "Harry Lorrequer," and some later novels of that sort, which did not help him on the subject required, yet took up all his time, so that he found himself unfitted for anything else when the examinations came. In consequence he was requested to leave.

Agamemnon always missed in his recitations, for the same reason that Elizabeth Eliza did not get on in school, because he was always asked the questions he did not know. It seemed provoking; if the professors had only asked something else! But they always hit upon the very things he had not studied up.

Mrs. Peterkin felt this was encouraging, for Agamemnon knew the things they did not know in colleges. In colleges they were willing to take for students only those who already knew certain things. She thought Agamemnon might be a professor in a college for those students who didn't know those things.

"I suppose these professors could not have known a great deal," she added, "or they would not have asked you so many questions; they would have told you something."

Agamemnon had left another college on account of

a mistake he had made with some of his classmates. They had taken a great deal of trouble to bring some wood from a distant wood-pile to make a bonfire with, under one of the professors' windows. Agamemnon had felt it would be a compliment to the professor.

It was with bonfires that heroes had been greeted on their return from successful wars. In this way beacon-lights had been kindled upon lofty heights, that had inspired mariners seeking their homes after distant adventures. As he plodded back and forward he imagined himself some hero of antiquity. He was reading " Plutarch's Lives " with deep interest. This had been recommended at a former college, and he was now taking it up in the midst of his French course. He fancied, even, that some future Plutarch was growing up in Lynn, perhaps, who would write of this night of suffering, and glorify its heroes.

For himself he took a severe cold and suffered from chilblains, in consequence of going back and forward through the snow, carrying the wood.

But the flames of the bonfire caught the blinds of the professor's room, and set fire to the building, and came near burning up the whole institution. Agamemnon regretted the result as much as his predecessor, who gave him his name, must have regretted that other bonfire, on the shores of Aulis, that deprived him of a daughter.

The result for Agamemnon was that he was requested to leave, after having been in the institution but a few months.

He left another college in consequence of a mis-understanding about the hour for morning prayers. He went every day regularly at ten o'clock, but found, after-ward, that he should have gone at half-past six. This hour seemed to him and to Mrs. Peterkin unseasonable, at a time of year when the sun was not up, and he would have been obliged to go to the expense of candles.

Agamemnon was always willing to try another college, wherever he could be admitted. He wanted to attain knowledge, however it might be found. But, after going to five, and leaving each before the year was out, he gave it up.

He determined to lay out the money that would have been expended in a collegiate education in buying an Encyclopædia, the most complete that he could find, and to spend his life studying it systematically. He would not content himself with merely reading it, but he would study into each subject as it came up, and perfect himself in that subject. By the time, then, that he had finished the Encyclopædia he should have embraced all knowledge, and have experienced much of it.

The family were much interested in this plan of making practice of every subject that came up.

He did not, of course, get on very fast in this way. In the second column of the very first page he met with A as a note in music. This led him to the study of music. He bought a flute, and took some lessons, and attempted to accompany Elizabeth Eliza on the piano. This, of course, distracted him from his work on the Encyclopædia. But he did not wish to return to A until he felt perfect in music. This required a long time.

Then in this same paragraph a reference was made; in it he was requested to "see Keys." It was necessary, then, to turn to "Keys." This was about the time the family were moving, which we have mentioned, when the difficult subject of keys came up, that suggested to him his own simple invention, and the hope of getting a patent for it. This led him astray, as inventions before have done with master-minds, so that he was drawn aside from his regular study.

The family, however, were perfectly satisfied with the career Agamemnon had chosen. It would help them all, in any path of life, if he should master the Encyclopædia in a thorough way.

Mr. Peterkin agreed it would in the end be not as expensive as a college course, even if Agamemnon should buy all the different Encyclopædias that appeared. There would be no "spreads" involved; no expense of receiving friends at entertainments in college; he could live at home, so that it would not be necessary to fit up another room, as at college. At all the times of his leaving he had sold out favorably to other occupants.

Solomon John's destiny was more uncertain. He was looking forward to being a doctor some time, but he had not decided whether to be allopathic or homœopathic.

or whether he could not better invent his own pills. And he could not understand how to obtain his doctor's degree.

For a few weeks he acted as clerk in a druggist's store. But he could serve only in the tooth-brush and soap department, because it was found he was not familiar enough with the Latin language to compound the drugs. He agreed to spend his evenings in studying the Latin grammar; but his course was interrupted by his being dismissed for treating the little boys too frequently to soda.

The little boys were going through the schools regularly. The family had been much exercised with regard to their education. Elizabeth Eliza felt that everything should be expected from them; they ought to take advantage from the family mistakes. Every new method that came up was tried upon the little boys. They had been taught spelling by all the different systems, and were  just able to read, when Mr. Peterkin learned that it was now considered best that children should not be taught to read till they were ten years old.

Mrs. Peterkin was in despair. Perhaps, if their books were taken from them even then, they might forget what they had learned. But no, the evil was done; the brain had received certain impressions that could not be blurred over.

This was long ago, however. The little boys had since entered the public schools. They went also to a gymnasium, and a whittling school, and joined a class in music, and another in dancing; they went to some afternoon lectures for children, when there was no other school, and belonged to a walking-club. Still Mr. Peter-

kin was dissatisfied by the slowness of their progress. He visited the schools himself, and found that they did not lead their classes. It seemed to him a great deal of time was spent in things that were not instructive, such as putting on and taking off their india-rubber boots.

Elizabeth Eliza proposed that they should be taken from school and taught by Agamemnon from the Encyclopædia. The rest of the family might help in the education at all hours of the day. Solomon John could take up the Latin grammar; and she could give lessons in French.

The little boys were enchanted with the plan, only they did not want to have the study-hours all the time.

Mr. Peterkin, however, had a magnificent idea, that they should make their life one grand Object Lesson. They should begin at breakfast, and study everything put upon the table, — the material of which it was made, and where it came from. In the study of the letter A, Agamemnon had embraced the study of music, and from one meal they might gain instruction enough for a day.

"We shall have the assistance," said Mr. Peterkin, "of Agamemnon, with his Encyclopædia."

Agamemnon modestly suggested that he had not yet got out of A, and in their first breakfast everything would therefore have to begin with A.

"That would not be impossible," said Mr. Peterkin. "There is Amanda, who will wait on table, to start with " —

"We could have 'am-and-eggs," suggested Solomon John.

Mrs. Peterkin was distressed. It was hard enough to think of anything for breakfast, and impossible if it all had to begin with one letter.

Elizabeth Eliza thought it would not be necessary. All they were to do was to ask questions, as in examination papers, and find their answers as they could. They could still apply to the Encyclopædia, even if it were not in Agamemnon's alphabetical course.

Mr. Peterkin suggested a great variety. One day they would study the botany of the breakfast-table; another day, its natural history. The study of butter would include that of the cow. Even that of the butter-dish would bring in geology. The little boys were charmed at the idea of learning pottery from the cream-jug, and they were promised a potter's wheel directly.

"You see, my dear," said Mr. Peterkin to his wife,

"before many weeks we shall be drinking our milk from jugs made by our children."

Elizabeth Eliza hoped for a thorough study.

"Yes," said Mr. Peterkin, "we might begin with botany. That would be near to Agamemnon alphabetically. We ought to find out the botany of butter. On what does the cow feed?"

The little boys were eager to go out and see.

"If she eats clover," said Mr. Peterkin, "we shall expect the botany of clover."

The little boys insisted that they were to begin the next day; that very evening they should go out and study the cow.

Mrs. Peterkin sighed, and decided she would order a simple breakfast. The little boys took their note-books and pencils, and clambered upon the fence, where they seated themselves in a row.

For there were three little boys. So it was now supposed. They were always coming in or going out, and it had been difficult to count them, and nobody was very sure how many there were.

There they sat, however, on the fence, looking at the cow. She looked at them with large eyes.

"She won't eat," they cried, "while we are looking at her!"

So they turned about, and pretended to look into the street, and seated themselves that way, turning their heads back, from time to time, to see the cow.

"Now she is nibbling a clover."

"No, that is a bit of sorrel."

"It's a whole handful of grass."

"What kind of grass?" they exclaimed.

It was very hard, sitting with their backs to the cow, and pretending to the cow that they were looking into the street, and yet to be looking at the cow all the time, and finding out what she was eating; and the upper rail of the fence was narrow and a little sharp. It was very high, too, for some additional rails had been put on to prevent the cow from jumping into the garden or street.

Suddenly, looking out into the hazy twilight, Elizabeth Eliza saw six legs and six india-rubber boots in the air, and the little boys disappeared!

"They are tossed by the cow! The little boys are tossed by the cow!"

Mrs. Peterkin rushed for the window, but fainted on the way. Solomon John and Elizabeth Eliza were hurrying to the door, but stopped, not knowing what to do next. Mrs. Peterkin recovered herself with a supreme effort, and sent them out to the rescue.

But what could they do? The fence had been made so high, to keep the cow out, that nobody could get in. The boy that did the milking had gone off with the key of the outer gate, and perhaps with the key of the shed door. Even if that were not locked, before Agamemnon could get round by the wood-shed and cow-shed, the little boys might be gored through and through!

Elizabeth Eliza ran to the neighbors, Solomon John to the druggist's for plasters, while Agamemnon made his way through the dining-room to the wood-shed and outer-shed door. Mr. Peterkin mounted the outside of the fence, while Mrs. Peterkin begged him not to put himself in danger. He climbed high enough to view the scene. He held to the corner post and reported what he saw.

They were not gored. The cow was at the other end of the lot. One of the little boys was lying in a bunch of dark leaves. He was moving.

The cow glared, but did not stir. Another little boy was pulling his india-rubber boots out of the mud. The cow still looked at him.

Another was feeling the top of his head. The cow began to crop the grass, still looking at him.

Agamemnon had reached and opened the shed-door. The little boys were next seen running toward it.

A crowd of neighbors, with pitchforks, had returned meanwhile with Elizabeth Eliza. Solomon John had brought four druggists. But, by the time they had reached the house, the three little boys were safe in the arms of their mother!

"This is too dangerous a form of education," she cried; "I had rather they w nt to school."

"No!" tney bravely cried. They were still willing to try the other way.

THE EDUCATIONAL BREAKFAST.

RS. PETERKIN'S nerves were so shaken by the excitement of the fall of the three little boys into the enclosure where the cow was kept that the educational breakfast was long postponed. The little boys continued at school, as before, and the conversation dwelt as little as possible upon the subject of education.

Mrs. Peterkin's spirits, however, gradually recovered. The little boys were allowed to watch the cow at her feed. A series of strings was arranged by Agamemnon and Solomon John, by which the little boys could be pulled up, if they should again fall down into the enclosure. These were planned something like curtain-cords, and Solomon John frequently amused himself by pulling one of the little boys up or letting him down.

Some conversation did again fall upon the old difficulty of questions. Elizabeth Eliza declared that it was not always necessary to answer; that many who could did not answer questions, — the conductors of the railroads, for instance, who probably knew the names of all the stations on a road, but were seldom able to tell them.

"Yes," said Agamemnon, "one might be a conductor without even knowing the names of the stations, because you can't understand them when they do tell them!"

"I never know," said Elizabeth Eliza, "whether it is ignorance in them, or unwillingness, that prevents them from telling you how soon one station is coming, or how long you are to stop, even if one asks ever so many times. It would be so useful if they would tell."

Mrs. Peterkin thought this was carried too far in the horse-cars in Boston. The conductors had always left you as far as possible from the place where you wanted  to stop; but it seemed a little too much to have the aldermen take it up, and put a notice in the cars, ordering the conductors "to stop at the farthest crossing."

Mrs. Peterkin was, indeed, recovering her spirits. She had been carrying on a brisk correspondence with Philadelphia, that she had imparted to no one, and at last she announced, as its result, that she was ready for a breakfast on educational principles.

A breakfast indeed, when it appeared! Mrs. Peterkin had mistaken the alphabetical suggestion, and had grasped the idea that the whole alphabet must be represented in one breakfast.

This, therefore, was the bill of fare: Apple-sauce, Bread, Butter, Coffee, Cream, Doughnuts, Eggs, Fish-balls, Griddles, Ham, Ice (on butter), Jam, Krout (sour), Lamb-chops, Morning Newspapers, Oatmeal, Pepper, Quince-marmalade, Rolls, Salt, Tea Urn, Veal-pie, Waffles, Yeast-biscuit.

Mr. Peterkin was proud and astonished. "Excellent!" he cried. "Every letter represented except Z." Mrs. Peterkin drew from her pocket a letter from the lady from Philadelphia. "She thought you would call it X-cellent for X, and she tells us," she read, "that if you come with a zest, you will bring the Z."

Mr. Peterkin was enchanted. He only felt that he ought to invite the children in the primary schools to such a breakfast; what a zest, indeed, it would give to the study of their letters!

It was decided to begin with Apple-sauce.

"How happy," exclaimed Mr. Peterkin, "that this should come first of all! A child might be brought up on apple-sauce till he had mastered the first letter of the alphabet, and could go on to the more involved subjects hidden in bread, butter, baked beans, etc."

Agamemnon thought his father hardly knew how much was hidden in the apple. There was all the story of William Tell and the Swiss independence. The little boys were wild to act William Tell, but Mrs. Peterkin was afraid of the arrows. Mr. Peterkin proposed they should begin by eating the apple-sauce, then discussing it, first botanically, next historically; or perhaps first historically, beginning with Adam and Eve, and the first apple.

Mrs. Peterkin feared the coffee would be getting cold, and the griddles were waiting. For herself, she declared she felt more at home on the marmalade, because the quinces came from grandfather's, and she had seen them planted; she remembered all about it, and now the bush came up to the sitting-room window. She seemed to have heard him tell that the town of Quincy, where the granite came from, was named from them, and she never quite recollected why, except they were so hard, as hard as stone, and it took you almost the whole day to stew them, and then you might as well set them on again.

Mr. Peterkin was glad to be reminded of the old place at grandfather's. In order to know thoroughly about apples they ought to understand the making of cider. Now, they might some time drive up to grandfather's, scarcely twelve miles away, and see the cider made. Why, indeed, should not the family go this very day up to grandfather's and continue the education of the breakfast?

"Why not, indeed?" exclaimed the little boys. A day at grandfather's would give them the whole process of the apple, from the orchard to the cider-mill. In this way they could widen the field of study, even to follow in time the cup of coffee to Java.

It was suggested, too, that at grandfather's they

might study the processes of maple syrup as involved in the griddle-cakes.

Agamemnon pointed out the connection between the two subjects: they were both the products of trees, — the apple-tree and the maple. Mr. Peterkin proposed that the lesson for the day should be considered the study of trees, and on the way they could look at other trees.

Why not, indeed, go this very day? There was no time like the present. Their breakfast had been so copious they would scarcely be in a hurry for dinner, and would, therefore, have the whole day before them.

Mrs. Peterkin could put up the remains of the breakfast for luncheon.

But how should they go? The carryall, in spite of its name, could hardly take the whole family, though they might squeeze in six, as the little boys did not take up much room.

Elizabeth Eliza suggested that she could spend the night at grandfather's. Indeed, she had been planning a visit there, and would not object to staying some days. This would make it easier about coming home, but it did not settle the difficulty in getting there.

Why not "Ride and Tie"?

The little boys were fond of walking; so was Mr

Peterkin; and Agamemnon and Solomon John did not object to their turn. Mrs. Peterkin could sit in the carriage, when it was waiting for the pedestrians to come up; or, she said, she did not object to a little turn of walking. Mr. Peterkin would start, with Solomon John and the little boys, before the rest, and Agamemnon should drive his mother and Elizabeth Eliza to the first stopping-place.

Then came up another question, — of Elizabeth Eliza's trunk. If she stayed a few days she would need to carry something. It might  be hot, and it might be cold. Just as soon as she carried her thin things she would need her heaviest wraps. You never could depend upon the weather. Even "Probabilities" got you no farther than to-day.

In an inspired moment Elizabeth Eliza bethought herself of the expressman. She would send her trunk by the express, and she left the table directly to go and pack it. Mrs. Peterkin busied herself with Amanda over the remains of the breakfast. Mr. Peterkin and Agamemnon went to order the horse and the expressman, and Solomon John and the little boys prepared themselves for a pedestrian excursion.

Elizabeth Eliza found it difficult to pack in a hurry; there were so many things she might want, and then again she might not. She must put up her music, because her grandfather had a piano; and then she bethought herself of Agamemnon's flute, and decided to pick out a volume or two of the Encyclopædia. But it was hard to decide, all by herself, whether to take G for griddle-cakes, or M for maple-syrup, or T for tree. She would take as many as she could make room for. She put up her work-box and two extra work-baskets, and she must take some French books she had never yet found time to read. This involved taking her French dictionary, as she doubted if her grandfather had one. She ought to put in a "Botany," if they were to study trees; but she could not tell which, so she would take all there were. She might as well take all her dresses, and it was no harm if one had too many wraps. When she had her trunk packed she found it over-full; it was difficult to

shut it. She had heard Solomon John set out from the front door with his father and the little boys, and Agamemnon was busy holding the horse at the side door, so there was no use in calling for help. She got upon the trunk; she jumped upon it; she sat down upon it, and, leaning over, found she could lock it! Yes, it was really locked.

But, on getting down from the trunk, she found her dress had been caught in the lid; she could not move away from it! What was worse, she was so fastened to the trunk that she could not lean forward far enough to turn the key back, to unlock the trunk and release herself! The lock had slipped easily, but she could not now get hold of the key in the right way to turn it back.

She tried to pull her dress away. No, it was caught too firmly. She called for help to her mother or Amanda, to come and open the trunk. But her door was shut. Nobody near enough to hear! She tried to pull the trunk toward the door, to open it and make herself heard; but it was so heavy that, in her constrained position, she could not stir it. In her agony she would have been willing to have torn her dress; but it was her travelling dress, and too stout to tear. She might cut it carefully. Alas, she had packed her scissors, and her knife she had lent to the little boys the day before! She called again. What silence there was in the house! Her voice seemed to echo through the room. At length, as she listened, she heard the sound of wheels.

Was it the carriage, rolling away from the side door? Did she hear the front door shut? She remembered then that Amanda was to "have the day." But she, Elizabeth Eliza, was to have spoken to Amanda, to explain to her to wait for the expressman. She was to have told her as she went downstairs. But she had not been able to go downstairs! And Amanda must have supposed that all the family had left, and she, too, must have gone, knowing nothing of the expressman. Yes, she heard the wheels! She heard the front door shut!

But could they have gone without her? Then she recalled that she had proposed walking on a little way with Solomon John and her father, to be picked up by Mrs. Peterkin, if she should have finished her packing in time. Her mother must have supposed that she had done so, — that she had spoken to Amanda, and started with the rest. Well, she would soon discover her mistake. She would overtake the walking party, and, not finding Elizabeth Eliza, would return for her. Patience only was needed. She had looked around for something to read; but she had packed up all her books. She had packed her knitting. How quiet and still it was! She tried to imagine where her mother would meet the rest of the family. They were good walkers, and they might have reached the two-mile bridge. But suppose they should stop for water beneath the arch of the bridge, as they often did, and the carryall pass over it without seeing them, her mother would not know but she was with them? And suppose her mother should decide to leave the horse at the place proposed for stopping and waiting for the first pedestrian party, and herself walk on, no one would be left to tell the rest when they should come up to the carryall. They might go on so, through the whole journey, without meeting, and she might not be missed till they shou'd reach her grandfather's!

Horrible thought! She would be left here alone all day. The expressman would come, but the expressman would go, for he would not be able to get into the house! She thought of the terrible story of Ginevra, of the

bride who was shut up in her trunk, and forever! She
was shut up on hers, and knew not when she should be
released! She had acted once in the ballad of the
"Mistletoe Bough." She had been one of the "guests,"
who had sung "Oh, the Mistletoe Bough!" and had looked
up at it, and she had seen at the side-scenes
how the bride had laughingly stepped into
the trunk. But the trunk then was only a
make-believe of some boards in front of a
sofa, and this was a stern reality.

It would be late now before her family
would reach her grandfather's. Perhaps
they would decide to spend the night. Perhaps they would fancy she was coming by
express. She gave another tremendous
effort to move the trunk toward the door. In vain.
All was still.

Meanwhile, Mrs. Peterkin sat some time at the door,
wondering why Elizabeth Eliza did not come down. Mr.
Peterkin had started on, with Solomon John and all the

little boys. Agamemnon had
packed the things into the
carriage, — a basket of lunch,
a change of shoes for Mr.
Peterkin, some extra wraps,
— everything that Mrs.
Peterkin could think of for the family comfort. Still
Elizabeth Eliza did not come. "I think she must have

walked on with your father," she said, at last; "you had better get in." Agamemnon now got in. "I should think she would have mentioned it," she continued; "but we may as well start on, and pick her up!" They started off. "I hope Elizabeth Eliza thought to speak to Amanda, but we must ask her when we come up with her."

But they did not come up with Elizabeth Eliza. At the turn beyond the village they found an envelope stuck up in an inviting manner against a tree. In this way they had agreed to leave missives for each other as they passed on. This note informed them that the walking party was going to take the short cut across the meadows, and would still be in front of them. They saw the party at last, just beyond the short cut; but Mr. Peterkin was explaining the character of the oak-tree to his children as they stood around a large specimen.

"I suppose he is telling them that it is some kind of a ' *Quercus,*'" said Agamemnon, thoughtfully.

Mrs. Peterkin thought Mr. Peterkin would scarcely use such an expression; but she could see nothing of Elizabeth Eliza. Some of the party, however, were behind the tree, some were in front, and Elizabeth Eliza might be behind the tree. They were too far off to be shouted at. Mrs. Peterkin was calmed, and went on to the stopping-place agreed upon, which they reached before long. This had been appointed near Farmer Gordon's barn, that there might be somebody at hand whom they knew, in case there should be any difficulty in untying the horse. The plan had been that Mrs. Peterkin should always sit in the carriage, while the others should take turns for walking; and Agamemnon tied the horse to a fence, and left her comfortably arranged with her knitting. Indeed, she had risen so early to prepare for the alphabetical breakfast, and had since been so tired with preparations, that she was quite sleepy, and would not object to a nap in the shade, by the soothing sound of the buzzing of the flies. But she called Agamemnon back, as he started off for his solitary walk, with a perplexing question: —

"Suppose the rest all should arrive, how could they now be accommodated in the carryall? It would be too much for the horse! Why had Elizabeth Eliza gone with the rest without counting up? Of course, they must have expected that she — Mrs. Peterkin — would walk on to the next stopping-place!"

She decided there was no way but for her to walk on. When the rest passed her they might make a change. So she put up her knitting cheerfully. It was a little joggly in the carriage, she had already found, for the horse was restless from the flies, and she did not like being left alone.

She walked on then with Agamemnon. It was very pleasant at first, but the sun became hot, and it was not long before she was fatigued. When they reached a hay-field she proposed going in to rest upon one of the hay-cocks. The largest and most shady was at the other end of the field, and they were seated there when the carryall passed them in the road. Mrs. Peterkin waved parasol and hat, and the party in the carryall returned their greetings; but they were too far apart to hear each other.

Mrs. Peterkin and Agamemnon slowly resumed their walk.

"Well, we shall find Elizabeth Eliza in the carry-all," she said, "and that will explain all."

But it took them an hour or two to reach the carry-all, with frequent stoppings for rest, and when they reached it no one was in it. A note was pinned up in the vehicle to say they had all walked on; it was "prime fun."

In this way the parties continued to dodge each other, for Mrs. Peterkin felt that she must walk on from the next station, and the carryall missed her again while she and Agamemnon stopped in a house to rest, and for a glass of water. She reached the carryall to find again that no one was in it. The party had passed on for the last station, where it had been decided all should meet at the foot of grandfather's hill, that they might all arrive at the house together. Mrs. Peterkin and Aga-memnon looked out eagerly for the party all the way, as Elizabeth Eliza must be tired by this time; but Mrs. Peterkin's last walk had been so slow that the other party were far in advance and reached the stopping-place before them. The little boys were all rowed out on the stone fence, awaiting them, full of delight at having reached grandfather's. Mr. Peterkin came forward to meet them, and, at the same moment with Mrs. Peterkin, exclaimed: "Where is Elizabeth Eliza?" Each party looked eagerly at the other; no Elizabeth Eliza was to be seen. Where was she? What was to be done? Was she left behind? Mrs. Peterkin was convinced she must have somehow got to grandfather's. They hurried up the hill. Grandfather and all the family came out to greet them, for they had been seen approaching. There was great questioning, but no Elizabeth Eliza!

It was sunset; the view was wide and fine. Mr. and Mrs. Peterkin stood and looked out from the north to the south. Was it too late to send back for Elizabeth Eliza? Where was she?

Meanwhile the little boys had been informing the family of the object of their visit, and while Mr. and Mrs. Peterkin were looking up and down the road, and Agamemnon and Solomon John were explaining to each other the details of their journeys, they had discovered some facts.

"We shall have to go back," they exclaimed. "We are too late! The maple-syrup was all made last spring."

"We are too early; we shall have to stay two or three months, — the cider is not made till October."

The expedition was a failure! They could study the making of neither maple-syrup nor cider, and Elizabeth Eliza was lost, perhaps forever! The sun went down, and Mr. and Mrs. Peterkin still stood to look up and down the road.

. . . .

Elizabeth Eliza, meanwhile, had sat upon her trunk as it seemed, for ages. She recalled all the terrible stories of prisoners, — how they had watched the growth of flowers through cracks in the pavement. She wondered how long she could live without eating. How thankful she was for her abundant breakfast!

At length she heard the door-bell. But who could go to the door to answer it? In vain did she make another effort to escape; it was impossible!

How singular! — there were footsteps. Some one was going to the door; some one had opened it. "They must be burglars." Well, perhaps that was a better fate — to be gagged by burglars, and the neighbors informed — than to be forever locked on her trunk. The steps approached the door. It opened, and Amanda ushered in the expressman.

Amanda had not gone. She had gathered, while waiting at the breakfast-table, that there was to be an expressman whom she must receive.

Elizabeth Eliza explained the situation. The expressman turned the key of her trunk, and she was released!

What should she do next? So long a time had elapsed she had given up all hope of her family returning for her. But how could she reach them?

She hastily prevailed upon the expressman to take her along until she should come up with some of the family. At least she would fall in with either the walking party or the carryall, or she would meet them if they were on their return.

She mounted the seat with the expressman, and slowly they took their way, stopping for occasional parcels as they left the village.

But, much to Elizabeth Eliza's dismay, they turned off from the main road on leaving the village. She remonstrated, but the driver insisted he must go round by Millikin's to leave a bedstead. They went round by Millikin's, and then had further turns to make. Elizabeth Eliza explained that in this way it would be impossible for her to find her parents and family, and at last he proposed to take her all the way with her trunk. She remembered with a shudder that when she had first asked about her trunk he had promised it should certainly be delivered the next morning. Suppose they should have to be out all night? Where did express-carts spend the night? She thought of herself in a lone wood, in an express-wagon! She could scarcely bring herself to ask, before assenting, when he should arrive.

"He guessed he could bring up before night."

And so it happened that as Mr. and Mrs. Peterkin in the late sunset were looking down the hill, wondering what they should do about the lost Elizabeth Eliza, they saw an express wagon approaching. A female form sat upon the front seat.

"She has decided to come by express," said Mrs. Peterkin. "It is — it is — Elizabeth Eliza!"

THE PETERKINS AT THE "CARNIVAL OF AUTHORS" IN BOSTON.

———◆———

HE Peterkins were in quite a muddle (for them) about the carnival of authors, to be given in Boston. As soon as it was announced, their interests were excited, and they determined that all the family should go.

But they conceived a wrong idea of the entertainment, as they supposed that every one must go in costume. Elizabeth Eliza thought their lessons in the foreign languages would help them much in conversing in character.

As the carnival was announced early Solomon John thought there would be time to read up everything written by all the authors, in order to be acquainted with the characters they introduced. Mrs. Peterkin did not wish to begin too early upon the reading, for she was sure she should forget all that the different authors had written before the day came.

But Elizabeth Eliza declared that she should hardly have time enough, as it was, to be acquainted with all the authors. She had given up her French lessons, after taking six, for want of time, and had, indeed, concluded she had learned in them all she should need to know of that language. She could repeat one or two pages of phrases, and she was astonished to find how much she could understand already of what the French teacher said to her; and he assured her that when she went to Paris she could at least ask the price of gloves, or of some other things she would need, and he taught her, too, how to pronounce "*garçon*," in calling for more.

Agamemnon thought that different members of the family might make themselves familiar with different authors; the little boys were already acquainted with "Mother Goose." Mr. Peterkin had read the "Pickwick Papers," and Solomon John had actually seen Mr. Longfellow getting into a horse-car.

Elizabeth Eliza suggested that they might ask the Turk to give lectures upon the "Arabian Nights." Everybody else was planning something of the sort, to "raise funds" for some purpose, and she was sure they ought not to be behindhand. Mrs. Peterkin approved of this. It would be excellent if they could raise funds enough to pay for their own tickets to the carnival; then they could go every night.

Elizabeth Eliza was uncertain. She thought it was usual to use the funds for some object. Mr. Peterkin said that if they gained funds enough they might arrange a booth of their own, and sit in it, and take the carnival comfortably. But Agamemnon reminded him that none of the family were authors, and only authors had booths. Solomon John, indeed, had once started upon writing a book, but he was not able to think of anything to put in it, and nothing had occurred to him yet.

Mr. Peterkin urged him to make one more effort. If his book could come out before the carnival he could go as an author, and might have a booth of his own, and take his family.

But Agamemnon declared it would take years to become an author. You might indeed publish something, but you had to make sure that it would be read. Mrs. Peterkin, on the other hand, was certain that libraries were filled with books that never were read, yet authors had written them. For herself, she had not read half the books in their own library. And she was glad there was to be a Carnival of Authors, that she might know who they were.

Mr. Peterkin did not understand why they called them a "Carnival"; but he supposed they should find out when they went to it.

Mrs. Peterkin still felt uncertain about costumes. She proposed looking over the old trunks in the garret. They would find some suitable dresses there, and these would suggest what characters they should take. Elizabeth Eliza was pleased with this thought. She remembered an old turban of white mull muslin, in an old bandbox, and why should not her mother wear it?

Mrs. Peterkin supposed that she should then go as her own grandmother.

Agamemnon did not approve of this. Turbans are now worn in the East, and Mrs. Peterkin could go in some Eastern character. Solomon John thought she might be Cleopatra, and this was determined on. Among the treasures found were some old bonnets, of large size, with waving plumes. Elizabeth Eliza decided upon the largest of these.

She was tempted to appear as Mrs. Columbus, as Solomon John was to take the character of Christopher Columbus; but he was planning to enter upon the stage in a boat, and Elizabeth Eliza was a little afraid of sea-sickness, as he had arranged to be a great while finding the shore.

Solomon John had been led to take this character by discovering a coal-hod that would answer for a helmet; then, as Christopher Columbus was born in Genoa, he could use the phrases in Italian he had lately learned of his teacher.

As the day approached the family had their costumes prepared.

Mr. Peterkin decided to be Peter the Great. It seemed to him a happy thought, for the few words of Russian he had learned would come in play, and he was quite sure that his own family name made him kin to that of the great Czar. He studied up the life in the Encyclopædia, and decided to take the costume of a ship-builder. He visited the navy-yard and some of the docks; but none of them gave him the true idea of dress for ship-building in Holland or St. Petersburg. But he found a picture of Peter the Great, representing him in a broad-brimmed hat. So he assumed one that he found at a costumer's, and with Elizabeth Eliza's black water-proof was satisfied with his own appearance.

Elizabeth Eliza wondered if she could not go with her father in some Russian character. She would have to lay aside her large bonnet, but she had seen pictures of Russian ladies, with fur muffs on their heads, and she might wear her own muff.

Mrs. Peterkin, as Cleopatra, wore the turban, with a little row of false curls in front, and a white embroidered muslin shawl crossed over her black silk dress. The little boys thought she looked much like the picture of their great-grandmother. But doubtless Cleopatra resembled this picture, as it was all so long ago, so the rest of the family decided.

Agamemnon determined to go as Noah. The costume, as represented in one of the little boys' arks, was simple. His father's red-lined dressing gown, turned inside out, permitted it easily.

Elizabeth Eliza was now anxious to be Mrs. Shem, and make a long dress of yellow flannel, and appear with

Agamemnon and the little boys. For the little boys were to represent two doves and a raven. There were feather-dusters enough in the family for their costumes, which would be then complete with their india-rubber boots.

Solomon John carried out in detail his idea of Christopher Columbus. He had a number of eggs boiled hard to take in his pocket, proposing to repeat, through the evening, the scene of setting the egg on its end. He gave up the plan of a boat, as it must be difficult to carry one into town; so he contented himself by prac-tising the motion of landing by stepping up on a chair.

But what scene could Elizabeth Eliza carry out? If they had an ark, as Mrs. Shem she might crawl in and out of the roof constantly, if it were not too high. But Mr. Peterkin thought it as difficult to take an ark into town as Solomon John's boat.

The evening came. But with all their preparations they got to the hall late. The entrance was filled with a crowd of people, and, as they stopped at the cloak-room, to leave their wraps, they found themselves en-tangled with a number of people in costume coming out from a dressing-room below. Mr. Peterkin was much encouraged. They were thus joining the performers. The band was playing the "Wedding March" as they went upstairs to a door of the hall which opened upon one side of the stage. Here a procession was marching up the steps of the stage, all in costume, and entering be-hind the scenes.

"We are just in the right time," whispered Mr. Peterkin to his family; "they are going upon the stage; we must fall into line."

The little boys had their feather-dusters ready.

Some words from one of the managers made Mr. Peterkin understand the situation.

"We are going to be introduced to Mr. Dickens," he said.

"I thought he was dead!" exclaimed Mrs. Peterkin, trembling.

"Authors live forever!" said Agamemnon in her ear.

At this moment they were ushered upon the stage.

The stage manager glared at them, as he awaited their names for introduction, while they came up all unannounced, — a part of the programme not expected. But he uttered the words upon his lips, "Great Expectations;" and the Peterkin family swept across the stage with the rest: Mr. Peterkin costumed as Peter the Great, Mrs. Peterkin as Cleopatra, Agamemnon as Noah, Solomon John as Christopher Columbus, Elizabeth Eliza in yellow flannel as Mrs. Shem, with a large, old-fashioned bonnet on her head as Mrs. Columbus, and the little boys behind as two doves and a raven.

Across the stage, in face of all the assembled people, then following the rest down the stairs on the other side, in among the audience, they went; but into an audience not dressed in costume!

There were Ann Maria Bromwick and the Osbornes, — all the neighbors, — all as natural as though they were walking the streets at home, though Ann Maria did wear white gloves.

"I had no idea you were to appear in character," said Ann Maria to Elizabeth Eliza; "to what booth do you belong?"

"We are no particular author," said Mr. Peterkin.

"Ah, I see, a sort of varieties' booth," said Mr. Osborne.

"What is your character?" asked Ann Maria of Elizabeth Eliza.

"I have not quite decided," said Elizabeth Eliza. "I thought I should find out after I came here. The marshal called us 'Great Expectations.'"

Mrs. Peterkin was at the summit of bliss. "I have shaken hands with Dickens!" she exclaimed.

But she looked round to ask the little boys if they, too, had shaken hands with the great man, but not a little boy could she find.

They had been swept off in Mother Goose's train, which had lingered on the steps to see the Dickens reception, with which the procession of characters in costume had closed. At this moment they were dancing round the barberry bush, in a corner of the balcony in Mother Goose's quarters, their feather-dusters gayly waving in the air.

But Mrs. Peterkin, far below, could not see this, and

consoled herself with the thought, they should all meet on the stage in the grand closing tableau. She was bewildered by the crowds which swept her hither and thither. At last she found herself in the Whittier Booth, and sat a long time calmly there. As Cleopatra she seemed out of place, but as her own grandmother she answered well with its New England scenery.

Solomon John wandered about, landing in America whenever he found a chance to enter a booth. Once before an admiring audience he set up his egg in the centre of the Goethe Booth, which had been deserted by its committee for the larger stage.

Agamemnon frequently stood in the background of scenes in the Arabian Nights.

It was with difficulty that the family could be repressed from going on the stage whenever the bugle sounded for the different groups represented there.

Elizabeth Eliza came near appearing in the "Dream of Fair Women," at its most culminating point.

Mr. Peterkin found himself with the "Cricket on the Hearth," in the Dickens Booth. He explained that he was Peter the Great, but always in the Russian language, which was never understood.

Elizabeth Eliza found herself, in turn, in all the booths. Every manager was puzzled by her appearance, and would send her to some other, and she passed along, always trying to explain that she had not yet decided upon her character.

Mr. Peterkin came and took Cleopatra from the Whittier Booth.

"I cannot understand," he said, "why none of our friends are dressed in costume, and why we are."

"I rather like it," said Elizabeth Eliza, "though I should be better pleased if I could form a group with some one."

The strains of the minuet began. Mrs. Peterkin was anxious to join the performers. It was the dance of her youth.

But she was delayed by one of the managers on the steps that led to the stage.

"I cannot understand this company," he said, distractedly.

"They cannot find their booth," said another.

"That is the case," said Mr. Peterkin, relieved to have it stated.

"Perhaps you had better pass into the corridor," said a polite marshal.

They did this, and, walking across, found themselves in the refreshment-room. "This is the booth for us," said Mr. Peterkin.

"Indeed it is," said Mrs. Peterkin, sinking into a chair, exhausted.

At this moment two doves and a raven appeared, — the little boys, who had been dancing eagerly in Mother Goose's establishment, and now came down for ice-cream.

"I hardly know how to sit down," said Elizabeth

Eliza, "for I am sure Mrs. Shem never could. Still, as I do not know if I am Mrs. Shem, I will venture it."

Happily, seats were to be found for all, and they were soon arranged in a row, calmly eating ice-cream.

"I think the truth is," said Mr. Peterkin, "that we represent historical people, and we ought to have been fictitious characters in books. That is, I observe, what the others are. We shall know better another time."

"If we only ever get home," said Mrs. Peterkin, "I shall not wish to come again. It seems like being on the stage, sitting in a booth, and it is so bewildering, Elizabeth Eliza not knowing who she is, and going round and round in this way."

"I am afraid we shall never reach home," said Agamemnon, who had been silent for some time; "we may have to spend the night here. I find I have lost our checks for our clothes in the cloak-room!"

"Spend the night in a booth, in Cleopatra's turban!" exclaimed Mrs. Peterkin.

"We should like to come every night," cried the little boys.

"But to spend the night," repeated Mrs. Peterkin.

"I conclude the Carnival keeps up all night," said Mr. Peterkin.

"But never to recover our cloaks," said Mrs. Peterkin; "could not the little boys look round for the checks on the floors?"

She began to enumerate the many valuable things

that they might never see again. She had worn her large fur cape of stone-marten, — her grandmother's, — that Elizabeth Eliza had been urging her to have made into a foot-rug. Now how she wished she had! And there were Mr. Peterkin's new overshoes, and Agamemnon had brought an umbrella, and the little boys had their mittens. Their india-rubber boots, fortunately, they had on, in the character of birds. But Solomon John had worn a fur cap, and Elizabeth Eliza a muff. Should they lose all these valuables entirely, and go home in the cold without them? No, it would be better to wait till everybody had gone, and then look carefully over the floors for the checks; if only the little boys could know where Agamemnon had been, they were willing to look. Mr. Peterkin was not sure as they would have time to reach the train. Still, they would need something to wear, and he could not tell the time. He had not brought his watch. It was a Waltham watch, and he thought it would not be in character for Peter the Great to wear it.

At this moment the strains of "Home, Sweet Home" were heard from the band, and people were seen preparing to go.

"All can go home, but we must stay," said Mrs. Peterkin, gloomily, as the well-known strains floated in from the larger hall.

A number of marshals came to the refreshment-room, looked at them, whispered to each other, as the Peterkins sat in a row.

"Can we do anything for you?" asked one at last. "Would you not like to go?" He seemed eager they should leave the room.

Mr. Peterkin explained that they could not go, as they had lost the checks for their wraps, and hoped to find their checks on the floor when everybody was gone. The marshal asked if they could not describe what they had worn, in which case the loss of the checks was not so important, as the crowds had now almost left, and it would not be difficult to identify their wraps. Mrs. Peterkin eagerly declared she could describe every article.

It was astonishing how the marshals hurried them through the quickly deserted corridors, how gladly they recovered their garments! Mrs. Peterkin, indeed, was disturbed by the eagerness of the marshals; she feared they had some pretext for getting the family out of the hall. Mrs. Peterkin was one of those who never consent to be forced to anything. She would not be compelled to go home, even with strains of music. She whispered her suspicions to Mr. Peterkin; but Agamemnon came hastily up to announce the time, which he had learned from the clock in the large hall. They must leave directly if they wished to catch the latest train, as there was barely time to reach it.

Then, indeed, was Mrs. Peterkin ready to leave. If they should miss the train! If she should have to pass the night in the streets in her turban! She was the first to lead the way, and, panting, the family followed her, just in time to take the train as it was leaving the station.

The excitement was not yet over. They found in the train many of their friends and neighbors, returning also from the Carnival; so they had many questions put to them which they were unable to answer. Still Mrs. Peterkin's turban was much admired, and indeed the whole appearance of the family; so that they felt themselves much repaid for their exertions.

But more adventures awaited them. They left the train with their friends; but as Mrs. Peterkin and Elizabeth Eliza were very tired, they walked very slowly, and Solomon John and the little boys were sent on with the pass-key to open the door. They soon returned with the startling intelligence that it was not the right key, and they could not get in. It was Mr. Peterkin's office-key; he had taken it by mistake, or he might have dropped the house-key in the cloak-room of the Carnival.

"Must we go back?" sighed Mrs. Peterkin, in an exhausted voice. More than ever did Elizabeth Eliza regret that Agamemnon's invention in keys had failed to secure a patent!

It was impossible to get into the house, for Amanda had been allowed to go and spend the night with a friend, so there was no use in ringing, though the little boys had tried it.

"We can return to the station," said Mr. Peterkin; "the rooms will be warm, on account of the midnight train. We can, at least, think what we shall do next."

At the station was one of their neighbors, proposing to take the New York midnight train, for it was now after eleven, and the train went through at half-past.

"I saw lights at the locksmith's over the way, as I passed," he said; "why do not you send over to the young man there? He can get your door open for you. I never would spend the night here."

Solomon John went over to "the young man," who agreed to go up to the house as soon as he had closed the shop, fit a key, and open the door, and come back to them on his way home. Solomon John came back to the station, for it was now cold and windy in the deserted streets. The family made themselves as comfortable as possible by the stove, sending Solomon John out occasionally to look for the young man. But somehow Solomon John missed him; the lights were out in the locksmith's shop, so he followed along to the house, hoping to find him there. But he was not there! He came back to report. Perhaps the young man had opened the door and gone on home. Solomon John and Agamemnon went back together, but they could not get in. Where was the young man? He had lately come to town, and nobody knew where he lived, for on the return of Solomon John and Agamemnon it had been proposed to go to the house of the young man. The night was wearing on. The midnight train had come and gone. The passengers who

came and went looked with wonder at Mrs. Peterkin, nodding in her turban, as she sat by the stove, on a corner
of a long bench.   At last the station-master had to leave,
for a short rest.   He felt obliged to lock up the station,
but he promised to return at an early hour to release
them.

"Of what use," said Elizabeth Eliza, "if we cannot
even then get into our own house?"

Mr. Peterkin thought the matter appeared bad, if the
locksmith had left town.   He feared the young man might
have gone in, and helped himself to spoons, and left.
Only they should have seen him if he had taken the midnight train.   Solomon John thought he appeared honest.
Mr. Peterkin only ventured to whisper his suspicions, as
he did not wish to arouse Mrs. Peterkin, who still was
nodding in the corner of the long bench.

Morning did come at last.   The family decided to go
to their home; perhaps by
some effort in the early day-
light they might make an entrance.

On the way they met with
the night-policeman, returning
from his beat.   He stopped
when he saw the family.

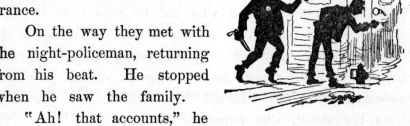

"Ah! that accounts," he
said; "you were all out last night, and the burglars took
occasion to make a raid on your house.   I caught a lively

young man in the very act; box of tools in his hand!
If I had been a minute late he would have made his
way in "—

The family then tried to interrupt — to explain—

"Where is he?" exclaimed Mr. Peterkin.

"Safe in the lock-up," answered the policeman.

"But he is the locksmith!" interrupted Solomon John

"We have no key!" said Elizabeth Eliza; "if you
have locked up the locksmith we can never get in."

The policeman looked from one to the other, smiling
slightly when he understood the case.

"The locksmith!" he exclaimed; "he is a new fellow,
and I did not recognize him, and arrested him! Very
well, I will go and let him out, that he may let you in!"
and he hurried away, surprising the Peterkin family with
what seemed like insulting screams of laughter.

"It seems to me a more serious case than it appears
to him," said Mr. Peterkin.

Mrs. Peterkin did not understand it at all. Had
burglars entered the house? Did the policeman say they
had taken spoons? And why did he appear so pleased?
She was sure the old silver teapot was locked up in the
closet of their room. Slowly the family walked towards
the house, and, almost as soon as they, the policeman
appeared with the released locksmith, and a few boys
from the street, who happened to be out early.

The locksmith was not in very good humor, and
took ill the jokes of the policeman. Mr. Peterkin, fear-

ing he might not consent to open the door, pressed into his hand a large sum of money. The door flew open; the family could go in. Amanda arrived at the same moment. There was hope of breakfast. Mrs. Peterkin staggered towards the stairs. "I shall never go to another Carnival!" she exclaimed.

THE PETERKINS AT THE FARM.

YES, at last they had reached the sea side, after much talking and deliberation, and summer after summer the journey had been constantly postponed.

But here they were at last, at the "Old Farm," so called, where seaside attractions had been praised in all the advertisements. And here they were to meet the Sylvesters, who knew all about the place, cousins of Ann Maria Bromwick. Elizabeth Eliza was astonished not to find them there, though she had not expected Ann Maria to join them till the very next day.

Their preparations had been so elaborate that at one time the whole thing had seemed hopeless; yet here they all were. Their trunks, to be sure, had not arrived; but the wagon was to be sent back for them, and, wonderful to tell, they had all their hand-baggage safe.

Agamemnon had brought his Portable Electrical Machine and Apparatus, and the volumes of the Encyclopædia that might tell him how to manage it, and Solomon John had his photograph camera. The little boys

had used their india-rubber boots as portmanteaux, filling
them to the brim, and carrying one in each hand, — a
very convenient way for travelling they considered it;
but they found on arriving (when they wanted to put
their boots directly on, for exploration round the house),
that it was somewhat inconvenient to have to begin to
unpack directly, and scarcely room enough could be found
for all the contents in the small chamber allotted to
them.

There was no room in the house for the electrical
machine and camera. Elizabeth Eliza thought the other
boarders were afraid of the machine going off; so an
out-house was found for them, where Agamemnon and
Solomon John could arrange them.

Mrs. Peterkin was much pleased with the old-fashioned
porch and low-studded rooms, though the sleeping-rooms
seemed a little stuffy at first.

Mr. Peterkin
was delighted
with the admira-
ble order in
which the farm
was evidently
kept. From the
first moment he
arrived he gave
himself to examining the well-stocked stables and barns,
and the fields and vegetable gardens, which were shown

to him by a highly intelligent person, a Mr. Atwood, who devoted himself to explaining to Mr. Peterkin all the details of methods in the farming.

The rest of the family were disturbed at being so far from the sea, when they found it would take nearly all the afternoon to reach the beach. The advertisements had surely stated that the "Old Farm" was directly on the shore, and that sea-bathing would be exceedingly convenient; which was hardly the case if it took you an hour and a half to walk to it.

Mr. Peterkin declared there were always such discrepancies between the advertisements of seaside places and the actual facts; but he was more than satisfied with the farm part, and was glad to remain and admire it, while the rest of the family went to find the beach, starting off in a wagon large enough to accommodate them, Agamemnon driving the one horse.

Solomon John had depended upon taking the photographs of the family in a row on the beach; but he decided not to take his camera out the first afternoon.

This was well, as the sun was already setting when they reached the beach.

"If this wagon were not so shaky," said Mrs. Peterkin, "we might drive over every morning for our bath. The road is very straight, and I suppose Agamemnon can turn on the beach."

"We should have to spend the whole day about it."

said Solomon John, in a discouraged tone, "unless we can have a quicker horse."

"Perhaps we should prefer that," said Elizabeth Eliza, a little gloomily, "to staying at the house."

She had been a little disturbed to find there were not more elegant and fashionable-looking boarders at the farm, and she was disappointed that the Sylvesters had not arrived, who would understand the ways of the place. Yet, again, she was somewhat relieved, for if their trunks did not come till the next day, as was feared, she should have nothing but her travelling dress to wear, which would certainly answer for to-night.

She had been busy all the early summer in preparing her dresses for this very watering-place, and, as far as appeared, she would hardly need them, and was disappointed to have no chance to display them. But of course, when the Sylvesters and Ann Maria came, all would be different; but they would surely be wasted on the two old ladies she had seen, and on the old men who had lounged about the porch; there surely was not a gentleman among them.

Agamemnon assured her she could not tell at the seaside, as gentlemen wore their exercise dress, and took a pride in going around in shocking hats and flannel suits. Doubtless they would be dressed for dinner on their return.

On their arrival they had been shown to a room to have their meals by themselves, and could not decide

whether they were eating dinner or lunch. There was a
variety of meat, vegetables, and pie, that might come
under either name; but Mr. and Mrs. Peterkin were well
pleased.

"I had no idea we should have really farm-fare," Mrs.
Peterkin said. "I have not drunk such a tumbler of milk
since I was young."

Elizabeth Eliza concluded they ought not to judge
from a first meal, as evidently their arrival had not been
fully prepared for, in spite of the numerous letters that
had been exchanged.

The little boys were, however, perfectly satisfied from
the moment of their arrival, and one of them had stayed
at the farm, declining to go to the beach, as he wished to
admire the pigs, cows, and horses; and all the way over
to the beach the other little boys were hopping in and
out of the wagon, which never went too fast, to pick
long mullein-stalks, for whips to urge on the reluctant horse
with, or to gather huckleberries, with which they were
rejoiced to find the fields were filled, although, as yet,
the berries were very green.

They wanted to stay longer on the beach, when they
finally reached it; but Mrs. Peterkin and Elizabeth Eliza
insisted upon turning directly back, as it was not fair to
be late to dinner the very first night.

On the whole the party came back cheerful, yet hungry.
They found the same old men, in the same costume, standing against the porch.

"A little seedy, I should say," said Solomon John.

"Smoking pipes," said Agamemnon; "I believe that is the latest style."

"The smell of their tobacco is not very agreeable," Mrs. Peterkin was forced to say.

There seemed the same uncertainty on their arrival as to where they were to be put, and as to their meals.

Elizabeth Eliza tried to get into conversation with the old ladies, who were wandering in and out of a small sitting-room. But one of them was very deaf, and the other seemed to be a foreigner. She discovered from a moderately tidy maid, by the name of Martha, who seemed a sort of factotum, that there were other ladies in their rooms, too much of invalids to appear.

"Regular bed-ridden," Martha had described them, which Elizabeth Eliza did not consider respectful.

Mr. Peterkin appeared coming down the slope of the hill behind the house, very cheerful. He had made the tour of the farm, and found it in admirable order.

Elizabeth Eliza felt it time to ask Martha about the next meal, and ventured to call it supper, as a sort of compromise between dinner and tea. If dinner were expected she might offend by taking it for granted that it was to be "tea," and if they were unused to a late dinner they might be disturbed if they had only provided a "tea."

So she asked what was the usual hour for supper, and was surprised when Martha replied, "The lady must say," nodding to Mrs. Peterkin. "She can have it just when she wants, and just what she wants!"

This was an unexpected courtesy.

Elizabeth Eliza asked when the others had their supper.

"Oh, they took it a long time ago," Martha answered. "If the lady will go out into the kitchen she can tell what she wants."

"Bring us in what you have," said Mr. Peterkin, himself quite hungry. "If you could cook us a fresh slice of beefsteak that would be well."

"Perhaps some eggs," murmured Mrs. Peterkin.

"Scrambled," cried one of the little boys.

"Fried potatoes would not be bad," suggested Agamemnon.

"Couldn't we have some onions?" asked the little boy who had stayed at home, and had noticed the odor of onions when the others had their supper.

"A pie would come in well," said Solomon John.

"And some stewed cherries," said the other little boy.

Martha fell to laying the table, and the family was much pleased, when, in the course of time, all the dishes they had recommended appeared. Their appetites were admirable, and they pronounced the food the same.

"This is true Arab hospitality," said Mr. Peterkin, as he cut his juicy beefsteak.

"I know it," said Elizabeth Eliza, whose spirits began to rise. "We have not even seen the host and hostess.'

She would, indeed, have been glad to find some one to tell her when the Sylvesters were expected, and why they had not arrived. Her room was in the wing, far from that of Mr. and Mrs. Peterkin, and near the aged deaf and foreign ladies, and she was kept awake for some time by perplexed thoughts.

She was sure the lady from Philadelphia, under such circumstances, would have written to somebody. But ought she to write to Ann Maria or the Sylvesters? And, if she did write, which had she better write to? She fully determined to write, the first thing in the morning, to both parties. But how should she address her letters? Would there be any use in sending to the Sylvesters' usual address, which she knew well by this time, merely to say they had not come? Of course the Sylvesters would know they had not come. It would be the same with Ann Maria. She might, indeed, inclose her letters to their several postmasters. Postmasters were always so obliging, and always knew where people were going to, and where to send their letters. She might, at least, write two letters, to say that they — the Peterkins — had arrived, and were disappointed not to find the Sylvesters. And she could add that their trunks had not arrived, and perhaps their friends might look out for them on their way. It really seemed a good plan to write. Yet another question came up, as to how she would get her letters to the post-office, as she had already learned it was at quite a distance, and in a different direction from the station, where they were to send the next day for their trunks.

She went over and over these same questions, kept awake by the coughing and talking of her neighbors, the other side of the thin partition.

She was scarcely sorry to be aroused from her uncomfortable sleep by the morning sounds of guinea-hens, peacocks, and every other kind of fowl.

Mrs. Peterkin expressed her satisfaction at the early breakfast, and declared she was delighted with such genuine farm sounds.

They passed the day much as the afternoon before, reaching the beach only in time to turn round to come back for their dinner, which was appointed at noon. Mrs. Peterkin was quite satisfied. "Such a straight road, and the beach such a safe place to turn round upon!"

Elizabeth Eliza was not so well pleased. A wagon had been sent to the station for their trunks, which could not be found; they were probably left at the Boston station, or, Mr. Atwood suggested, might have been switched off upon one of the White Mountain trains. There was no use to write any letters, as there was no way to send them. Elizabeth Eliza now almost hoped the Sylvesters would not come, for what should she do if the trunks did not come and all her new dresses? On her way over to the beach she had been thinking what she should do with her new foulard and cream-colored surah if the Sylvesters did not come, and if their time was spent in only driving to the beach and back. But now, she would prefer that the Sylvesters would not come till the dresses and the trunks did. All she could find out, from inquiry, on returning, was, "that another lot was expected on Saturday." The next day she suggested: —

"Suppose we take our dinner with us to the beach, and spend the day." The Sylvesters and Ann Maria then would find them on the beach, where her travelling-dress would be quite appropriate. "I am a little tired," she added, "of going back and forward over the same road; but when the rest come we can vary it."

The plan was agreed to, but Mr. Peterkin and the little boys remained to go over the farm again.

They had an excellent picnic on the beach, under the shadow of a ledge of sand. They were just putting up their things when they saw a party of people approaching from the other end of the beach.

"I am glad to see some pleasant-looking people at last," said Elizabeth Eliza, and they all turned to walk toward them.

As the other party drew near she recognized Ann Maria Bromwick! And with her were the Sylvesters, — so they proved to be, for she had never seen them before.

"What! you have come in our absence!" exclaimed Elizabeth Eliza.

"And we have been wondering what had become of you!" cried Ann Maria.

"I thought you would be at the farm before us,"

said Elizabeth Eliza to Mr. Sylvester, to whom she was introduced.

"We have been looking for you at the farm," he was saying to her.

"But we are at the farm," said Elizabeth Eliza.

"And so are we!" said Ann Maria.

"We have been there two days," said Mrs. Peterkin.

"And so have we, at the 'Old Farm,' just at the end of the beach," said Ann Maria.

"Our farm is old enough," said Solomon John.

"Whereabouts are you?" asked Mr. Sylvester.

Elizabeth Eliza pointed to the road they had come.

A smile came over Mr. Sylvester's face; he knew the country well.

"You mean the farm-house behind the hill, at the end of the road?" he asked.

The Peterkins all nodded affirmatively.

Ann Maria could not restrain herself, as broad smiles came over the faces of all the party.

"Why, that is the Poor-house!" she exclaimed.

"The town farm," Mr. Sylvester explained, deprecatingly.

The Peterkins were silent for a while. The Sylvesters tried not to laugh.

"There certainly were some disagreeable old men and women there!" said Elizabeth Eliza, at last.

"But we have surely been made very comfortable," Mrs. Peterkin declared.

"A very simple mistake," said Mr. Sylvester, continuing his amusement. "Your trunks arrived all right at the 'Old Farm,' two days ago."

"Let us go back directly," said Elizabeth Eliza.

"As directly as our horse will allow," said Agamemnon.

Mr. Sylvester helped them into the wagon. "Your rooms are awaiting you," he said. "Why not come with us?"

"We want to find Mr. Peterkin before we do anything else," said Mrs. Peterkin.

They rode back in silence, till Elizabeth Eliza said, "Do you suppose they took us for paupers?"

"We have not seen any 'they,'" said Solomon John, "except Mr. Atwood."

At the entrance of the farm-yard Mr. Peterkin met them.

"I have been looking for you," he said. "I have just made a discovery."

"We have made it, too," said Elizabeth Eliza; "we are in the poor-house."

"How did you find it out?" Mrs. Peterkin asked of Mr. Peterkin.

"Mr. Atwood came to me, puzzled with a telegram that had been brought to him from the station, which he ought to have got two days ago. It came from a Mr. Peters, whom they were expecting here this week, with his wife and boys, to take charge of the establishment.

He telegraphed to say he cannot come till Friday. Now, Mr. Atwood had supposed we were the Peterses, whom he had sent for the day we arrived, not having received this telegram."

"Oh, I see, I see!" said Mrs. Peterkin; "and we did get into a muddle at the station!"

Mr. Atwood met them at the porch. "I beg pardon," he said. "I hope you have found it comfortable here, and shall be glad to have you stay till Mr. Peters' family comes."

At this moment wheels were heard. Mr Sylvester had arrived, with an open wagon, to take the Peterkins to the "Old Farm."

Martha was waiting within the door, and said to Elizabeth Eliza, "Beg pardon, miss, for thinking you was one of the inmates, and putting you in that room. We thought it so kind of Mrs. Peters to take you off every day with the other gentlemen, that looked so wandering."

Elizabeth Eliza did not know whether to laugh or to cry.

Mr. Peterkin and the little boys decided to stay at the farm till Friday. But Agamemnon and Solomon John preferred to leave with Mr. Sylvester, and to take their electrical machine and camera when they came for Mr. Peterkin.

Mrs. Peterkin was tempted to stay another night, to be wakened once more by the guinea-hens. But Eliza-beth Eliza bore her off. There was not much packing to be done. She shouted good-by into the ears of the deaf old lady, and waved her hand to the foreign one, and glad to bid farewell to the old men with their pipes, leaning against the porch.

"This time," she said, "it is not our trunks that were lost" —

"But we, as a family," said Mrs. Peterkin.